The Moon is Real

Jerrod Edson

UFP Fiction Series
Detroit, Michigan, USA
Windsor, Ontario, Canada

Copyright 2016 by Jerrod Edson

No part of this book may be used or reproduced in any manner without written permission except in the case of brief quotations embodied in critical articles and reviews. Please direct all inquiries to: generalinquiries@urbanfarmhousepress.com

Published in the United States of America and Canada by

Urban Farmhouse Press
www.urbanfarmhousepress.com

First Edition. First Print Run.
July 2016

All Rights Reserved

ISBN: 978-1-988214-09-2

Book cover design: D.A. Lockhart
Book cover image: Lee D. Thompson
Book layout: D.A. Lockhart

The UFP Fiction Series is a line of books that showcases established and emerging voices from across North America. The books in this series represent what the editors at UFP believe to be some of the strongest voices in both American and Canadian fiction writing. *The Moon is Real* is the third book in this series.

Printed in Adobe Garamond Pro font

Contents

Chapter 1 /3
Chapter 2 /7
Chapter 3 /18
Chapter 4 /22
Chapter 5 /31
Chapter 6 /37
Chapter 7 /46
Chapter 8 /51
Chapter 9 /56
Chapter 10 /65
Chapter 11 /72
Chapter 12 /75
Chapter 13 /80
Chapter 14 /89
Chapter 15 /92
Chapter 16 /105
Chapter 17 /109
Chapter 18 /112
Chapter 19 /116
Chapter 20 /124
Chapter 21 /130
Chapter 22 /133
Chapter 23 /126

Thank You /143
About the Author /145

For Leigh, Hadley, and Harper

SMYTHE, EDWARD JAMES Jr. –

Unexpectedly at his home on Wednesday, March 30, 2011 at the age of 26. Born in Saint John, NB, in 1984, Eddie was predeceased by his parents Edward Smythe Sr. and Iris (Stephens) of Saint John. He is survived by his uncle Walter Stephens. Eddie was a longtime employee of Mel's Shoe Emporium. He had a passion for footwear.

Resting at Wiggins Funeral Home, 111 Paradise Row, Saint John, with visiting today from 6 to 9 PM. A private funeral service will be held on Sunday.

—Obituary in the *Telegraph-Journal*, Friday, April 1, 2011

Chapter 1

Charlie and Prin stood shivering in the empty parking lot outside Wiggins Funeral Home. It had snowed heavily during the day but now it was evening and the sky was clear and the moon was very bright. The lot had been plowed and salted in the afternoon but it was still covered in a fine layer of snow, with bare patches where the salt was thickest. From where Charlie and Prin stood they could see over the road and beyond the highway, to the black of the harbour and the lights of the Harbour Bridge arcing across it.

Prin flicked her cigarette onto the pavement.

"I hate cigarettes," she said.

"What do you think of all that in there?" Charlie asked.

"Oh, I don't know, Charles. I'm cold. I wish I hadn't come. Does it really matter that we stay?" She shivered. "It's all such a mess. That in there didn't even feel real to me. He looked like he was asleep."

"That's how he's supposed to look."

"It's just so creepy with the casket and all."

"Give me a smoke," Charlie said.

Prin dug into her purse and pulled out the pack.

"You're very good at this, Charles."

Charlie lit the cigarette and puffed.

A cold wind swept across the empty lot, a cold dampness that crept into their clothes. Prin crossed her arms and hopped on the spot.

"How long do we have to stand here?"

"I don't know," Charlie said. He offered his cigarette, and just then, a black Chrysler 300 with silver rims and blacked-out windows pulled into the lot. "That's them," he said.

Prin took a drag, a deep one, and exhaled.

"What do I do?"

"Act normal. Just talk to me—talk to me about Daisy."

"Okay," Prin said. She gave the cigarette back. "All she eats is pancakes and maple syrup but she's thin as a rail."

Charlie watched as the two men climbed out of the car and headed toward them.

"Real maple syrup?" He wanted Prin to keep talking.

Prin perked up.

"Well it's funny you should ask, because just yesterday I ran out and all I had was honey and she spit it out. She kept saying yucky, yucky! I'm telling you, she's spoilt rotten."

The two men glanced over at Charlie as they passed and climbed the steps to the front entrance. Charlie was relieved they didn't acknowledge him—that they hadn't noticed him, or didn't care to. He and Prin watched as they opened the door and went inside. For a short moment there was not a sound between them, just the swish of the passing cars on the wet road below.

"That was them?" Prin whispered.

"Yup."

"I've never seen real killers before."

Charlie started across the lot to his car.

"Well now you have."

A blue Ford Impala pulled into the lot and parked at the far end, backing under a cluster of bare lilac trees. Charlie immediately recognized it as an unmarked police cruiser—the black hubs on the wheels, the tiny antenna at the back, the two men who sat, looking at him. He took Prin by the arm.

"Let's get out of here."

✧

It was quiet inside the viewing room. The lights were dim. There was the smell of cleanliness, of newly-vacuumed carpet. The flowers placed about the room were leftovers from another wake, the petals losing their lustre in the pale light of the room. Eddie Smythe's friend Jeremy Wiggins had done the best he could, given the circumstances. It was Jeremy's family who owned Wiggins Funeral Home and he had re-used the flowers and had put on Eddie's wake free of charge.

Eddie's uncle Walter had been the first to arrive. He took off his winter jacket and folded it over his arm. He wore a tight blue sports coat and thin black tie and a toque with an Irving logo stitched onto the front. His nose was red from the cold. He nodded at Jeremy who greeted him upon entering, then spotted the casket across the room and walked cautiously toward it.

He took off his toque, clasping it with both hands, as though it were a prayer book. His hair was thin and white and with his toque off his nose looked very red. Two dimmed pot lights sent a subtle glow down upon the open casket, as though Eddie were angelic, that in death he'd become something special, something to be revered. But those who knew Eddie knew that he was far from it. But Walter did not know. He did not know enough of his nephew to think anything other than how angelic he looked under the lights. His eyes welled up, and he began to cry. Jeremy offered him a tissue. Walter wiped his eyes. He'd never made the effort with his nephew and now it was too late. Or was it? He pulled a framed portrait of Eddie's mother, Iris, from inside his sports coat and placed it in the casket, on Eddie's chest. Then he turned and walked over to one of the chairs against the outer wall, between two big windows, and sat.

Jeremy Wiggins stiffened and offered a nod and a courteous smile at the two men when they entered the room. These were the men from Montreal. These were Eddie's killers. It frightened him in such a way that he didn't know what to do, only that he should stand still and not do anything out of the ordinary, like stare or smile too much, or move at all. His legs felt pinned to the floor.

The two men went straight to the casket.

Jeremy watched as they hovered over the body.

The taller of the two stood with clasped hands, not awkwardly as Walter had with his toque, but stoically, professionally; this is what one did when paying respects, regardless if you put him there or not. His name was Ivan. He was very tall and had piercing grey eyes and slick black hair and wore an expensive black suit, tailored to fit his tall frame. He'd been awake for thirty-two hours and he yawned at the prospect of driving all the way back to Montreal tonight. His companion's name was Dmitri. He was nineteen years old and had boyish features—smooth skin and red cheeks. He was much shorter than Ivan but thicker in the chest, with a big head that sat low, as if his neck and shoulders were one, like a bull. He wore a black leather jacket and turtleneck that accentuated his frame. He was full of energy and could not stand still.

"And so here he is," Ivan said, his hands still clasped.

Dmitri sighed heavily through his nose.

"He's dead and it's clean," Ivan said. "That's all that matters."

Dmitri shook his head.

"It fuckin matters to me."

"Breathe," Ivan whispered.

Chapter 2

Two days before Eddie Smythe's wake the sun was shining on a very cold morning in Saint John. The sky was an open, endless blue. An icy wind from the bay swirled through the streets. The sidewalks were white with salt, and the streets too, dry and chalky white.

Prin lived in a two-bedroom apartment on Wentworth Street. It was an old building with ten-foot ceilings, crown molding, worn hardwood floors and a big bay window. Prin always had flowers in the bay window, which made her happy. Yesterday she bought a bouquet of tulips and she was pleased to see the sun shining through them. Toys were scattered throughout the apartment; dolls' clothes on the coffee table, pieces from a Hello Kitty puzzle on the floor. Her five-year-old daughter Daisy sat on the living room floor playing with a doll. She was built like her mother, awkward and skinny, with long thin legs and tiny arms and thin hair which fell flat down the sides of her face. But she had her mother's big blue eyes, and her mother's freckles, and she was a very cute little girl, the way she sat dressing her doll, legs crossed, focused, mouth closed and her tongue out. Prin often just sat and watched her play.

Later in the morning, they stepped out into the cold. The sun shone brightly upon the street.

"What a beautiful day," Prin smiled.

"It's cold!" Daisy said.

They were walking to the babysitter's, whose name was April, and who lived above a convenience store on Sydney Street. April cut hair in her apartment and it smelled of shampoo and cigarettes. She was middle-aged and had the voice of a smoker, cracked and coarse, and she was one of Prin's best friends.

Prin unzipped a backpack of dolls and dolls' clothes and spread them out on the living room floor where Daisy sat and started to play. Prin and April sat at the kitchen table.

"I was thinking of maybe taking Daisy over to King Square to feed the pigeons—if you think it's not too cold," April said.

"It's too cold!" Daisy said from the living room.

"It would be good for you to get some fresh air," Prin said.

Daisy's shoulders slumped, her face in a pout.

"What did we talk about the other day?" Prin said.

Daisy didn't answer.

"What did we talk about?"

"Be tough," Daisy said.

"Not just tough," Prin said. "Girl tough."

"Girl tough," April said. "I like that."

"It means you have to be tougher than a boy," Prin said. She looked at Daisy. "Right?"

Again Daisy didn't answer.

"Right?"

"Yes, mommy," Daisy said. She held up a doll she'd just stripped of its clothes. "I want to take Princess Fiona."

"Pick one for me too," April said. She turned to Prin. "You look tired."

"I am."

"How many do you have today?"

"Two," Prin said. She stood from the table and stepped into the living room, knelt beside Daisy and kissed her on the cheek. "Be good for April."

Prin didn't like working on such a beautiful day; she'd rather go to the park with Daisy and feed the pigeons. Daisy loved the pigeons. Oh, don't even start thinking of it, she told herself as she made her way down the narrow staircase and out onto Sydney Street. You make more money in a day what most make in a week. She passed through the salt-covered walkway at King Square, under the big oak trees and past the gazebo. She was saddened when she noticed a few pigeons pecking at the ground around an empty bench; she hated missing out on anything with Daisy.

She entered Brunswick Square Shopping Centre which occupied the first three floors of the Office Tower, a nineteen-floor office building in the heart of uptown. She took the escalator down to the first floor, to the washrooms past the eatery. She found an empty stall and put the toilet seat down. There was piss on the floor and she had to balance herself with one hand on the door to avoid stepping in it, while stripping out of her jogging pants and t-shirt. She hated this part, bumping her elbows in the tiny space, her bare legs touching the cold of the toilet. She dug into her bag for a mini-skirt, black nylons and black halter-top and flung them over the door. She pulled out her high-heeled shoes and nearly fell as she stood on one leg trying to get them on.

She stepped out of the stall and stood in front of the mirror and applied a thick layer of eyeliner. Then she puckered her lips and applied a glossy lipstick which made her lips look wet and full. Then she stepped out of the washroom, covered up by her winter jacket, an entirely different woman. Even her walk was different, an exaggerated swagger. It was all in the walk. It said: I know what I'm doing and where I'm going and to hell with everyone else. But if you looked closely you would see that she did not walk in perfect rhythm, the conscious effort it took to achieve the swagger threw off her step, but just a little, and only if you looked closely.

She made her way back up the escalator and out the doors to Germain Street, where she skipped up the sidewalk, her heels click-clacking on the frozen pavement. She climbed the steps of the office building, the tallest building in the city, and stepped into the elevator and hit the button for the fifteenth floor. She felt the plush of the carpet under her heels as she entered the foyer where the secretary sat, looking up at Prin. Prin liked the feeling of the carpet under her feet.

"I have an appointment with Mr. Cleary," she said.

"It's Prin, right?"

Prin nodded.

"You're a bit early," the secretary said. "Please, have a seat."

Prin smiled and sat. She liked the secretary, how nicely she always treated her, how professional she always was. We'd make good friends, she thought, watching as the secretary pushed a button on the phone and spoke into her headset.

"Mr. Cleary, Prin is here." She looked over at Prin. "He'll be just a minute."

Prin smiled again.

"We always have our meetings the same time every week." She did not know why she said this, but she regretted it right away.

"Yes, I know," the secretary said.

Prin bit her lip.

The secretary leaned forward to speak. Prin leaned forward to listen.

"Mr. Cleary has two granddaughters who are eighteen months old—twins, and cute as little buttons." She winked and lowered her voice. "I just thought you'd like to know that before you go in there and do whatever it is you do to him."

Prin sat back in the chair and stared at the wall and tried very hard not to cry. How was it that this woman was sitting there and Prin was where she was? She tried to think of something else, still staring at the wall, and so she thought of Daisy, of the first time she'd realized she was pregnant, of how she hadn't worried about it, hadn't suspected anything until she'd calculated that she was seven weeks late. And even then she'd denied it. Her body hadn't felt any different; there was never any sickness or weird cravings or anything like that. But when another three weeks came and went she started to worry. She went to Shoppers and bought a pregnancy test. It was awkward squatting over the toilet and reaching underneath and trying to pee on the stick and feeling the pee warm on her fingers. The + sign showed up immediately, a clear and solid blue. She grabbed the box and checked again to see what the + sign meant, even though she already knew. She called April right away.

"Calm down," April had said. "I know a clinic."

Prin was shaking her head.

"It's not that—that never crossed my mind." April was silent on the other end. Prin was still shaking her head. "It just doesn't seem right, with a baby inside me—to expose my baby to that—to do what I do. But I can't afford to live if I do anything else." She'd sighed heavily into the phone.

She was thinking of the money; how she'd taken a job at Sobeys for ten dollars an hour and moved to Millidgeville; that her savings had dwindled but she'd stayed true to her word; she hadn't worked another minute while Daisy was growing inside her; that she'd protected her like a good mother; that she went back to work two months after Daisy was born, telling herself it was worth it. She was thinking of all these things while still staring at the wall, trying not to cry, when the secretary spoke again.

"Mr. Cleary will see you now."

Prin could not look at her, could not thank her as she walked past the desk. All she could think of were Mr. Cleary's two grandchildren—that they were as cute as little buttons. The plush carpet did not feel nice anymore.

She opened the double doors and stepped inside. Mr. Cleary was sitting in his chair behind his desk, talking on the phone. He did not acknowledge her. Prin smelled the dark wood of the coffee table. She'd been in this office several times, and every time she smelled that coffee table it took her somewhere; it smelled exotic; none of the furniture in her apartment smelled like this. It was a large office, with a sitting area with a big comfortable couch and two chairs facing each other. In the middle was the coffee table, made of oak and stained dark and worn smooth, like a pew in an old church. Underneath it was a deep red Persian rug with an intricate floral design. On the wall behind the couch was a huge print of a panther. Prin quite liked the panther and how it blended darkly into the picture, and how the reds in the rug and the smell of the table all felt so warm and cozy and did not feel at all as though they were on the fifteenth floor of a building in the middle of the city.

Behind Mr. Cleary's desk were ceiling-to-wall windows that stretched the width of the office. From up here Prin could see the smoking rooftops of all the buildings between Canterbury and Germain Street, all the way to where the streets rose then dipped at Water Street and the Courtney Bay. She could see across the bay too, to the refineries at the industrial park, grey in the distance, and the hills beyond, the trees so far away they looked more black than green. The hills reminded her of the panther print and she wondered what animals were hiding among those tiny black trees so far away. If I worked here I'd look out that window all day, she thought. She liked seeing the bareness of the rooftops, the flatness of them from this point of view. They reminded her of that summer afternoon long ago when she'd sat up on a roof on Orange Street in her underwear drinking Corona, and out in the bay was an Irving Oil tanker, and closer, a cruise ship, gigantic and white as it made its way slowly out to sea. She wished she could get that afternoon back, and the night too—the night Daisy was conceived. But it was all so long ago it didn't seem real anymore, especially now, in this office as she stood a few feet beyond the doors, waiting. Everything was all so far away from her now.

Mr. Cleary hung up the phone and coughed to clear his throat. He was a heavy-set man, his skin sagging under his cheeks, his neckline damp with sweat. He wore a pin-stripe suit with a blue silk tie and it was only because he paid more than anyone else that Prin agreed to see him every week; his sweatiness repulsed her, and how he always cleared his throat—a hoarse gargle, the sound of someone being choked.

"Have a seat," he said, clearing his throat again. He loosened his tie and lumbered over to her. "Take off your panties—but leave the skirt on."

Prin sat on the couch and removed her panties and placed them on the coffee table. Her mind was on that Orange Street rooftop. How lovely it was taking the first sips of Corona and catching the bits of lime on your tongue, she thought. And the sun so warm on your skin and everything so perfect; how it is when you've just taken your first drink and the sun hits you and makes you feel alive and full of hope and you get a rumble in your belly because you feel happy all through your body and there's still all the night ahead.

"Rub your tits," Mr. Cleary said.

She squeezed her breasts together, her small, taut breasts. The bits of lime tickling your tongue, she thought. And Charlie sitting next to you and the sun is so high up and the sky is so blue and then a warm glow of hope sweeps over your whole body and settles into your chest and you feel that rumble of happiness again.

"Now down there," Mr. Cleary said. "Rub it too."

Just look how white the cruise ship is against the water, how the water sparkles in the sunlight.

"There, right there—keep doing that—yes, that's it."

And then in the evening making love on the floor, the very moment Daisy is conceived, and knowing you've made love truly, beautifully, for the first and only time in your life.

"Turn around."

She twisted herself around, on her knees, holding onto the back of the couch. She felt Mr. Cleary's clammy hands flip her skirt up over her buttocks, onto the small of her back, and the coolness of the office air between her legs as he entered her. And there was still the afternoon on the roof with the sunlight and the ships out on the bay and then the night and the most precious gift of Daisy nine months later and how you love that little girl so much that just thinking of her makes you glow, and she's smiling and laughing now with April, sitting in the park not two blocks away with her doll, Princess Fiona, feeding the pigeons. I wonder what doll Daisy chose for April—maybe Lady Buttercup, with the bright pink dress with the pretty little flowers.

He smacked her hard on the ass.

"Do you like that?"

Yes, Lady Buttercup and the bright pink—

He smacked her again, harder, and it stung.

"I said do you like that?"

"Ooh yeah, that feels good," she moaned, feeling the coldness of his hands pressing on her buttocks, pulling at her hips. She could hear the sweat in his voice, the smacking of his belly against her, the smell of coffee on his breath, the slimy wetness of his tongue as he ran it up the swell of her back and between her shoulders and then lifted the hair from off her neck and kissed her skin and ran his tongue up her neck and into her hairline.

"Take it then," he moaned into her ear.

He began to thrust harder, faster, each thrust a sweaty moan, a bluntness.

"Is this how you want it? Like this? Is it? Tell me it is. Tell me this is how you want it."

"Oh baby," Prin said.

The sunlight, the blueness of the sky—don't go don't go don't go.

"Oh yeah," he moaned. "This is how you like it, isn't it?"

He withdrew from her and lifted himself a little.

"No—not there—" Prin said. "Stop—please!"

It felt like being stabbed.

She tried to pull away but he gripped her tightly, his fingers like talons, locked into her shoulders and pressing down hard so that she couldn't move.

"Ah—you like it there, right there..."

Prin's eyes welled up and there was just the here and now, the right here and right now and nothing else, nothing else but the office and the couch and the hard thrusts like daggers into her; the sunlight and the water and the park and the pigeons and Lady Buttercup nowhere, no matter how hard she tried to find them, they were gone.

Mr. Cleary's grip tightened, his body stiffened, then he released his talons and slipped out of her.

Prin curled up on the couch, unable to move. She took quick short breaths, trying to control the pain as it throbbed and scraped. She was bleeding—she could feel it trickling out of her.

"Come and get your money," Mr. Cleary said, and cleared his throat.

She looked across the room and saw him straightening his tie in the gold reflection of a plaque on the wall. And then something in her erupted, an anger that came from the pain, and she got up and headed for him.

She came so fast Mr. Cleary did not have time to turn and see her, the pointed heel of her shoe hitting the side of his head with a sharp thud, then another as he dropped to the floor. With all her strength she kicked him in the ribs and he lurched sideways, gasping, curling into a clump. She knelt beside him, reached into his jacket for his wallet and grabbed the cash.

She still had only one shoe on when she hobbled past the secretary and slapped a few bills on the desk.

"Go get something for those grandkids," she said without stopping.

She went straight home, not changing her clothes, her short skirt showing the vein of blood running down the inside of her leg and into her shoe.

She ran the shower so hot she could barely stand it. Be tough, she told herself. It's nothing—you've been in this sort of thing before. No—it was never like this. No-one has ever done that. They've asked—almost all of them have asked—but you said no and it was done. A thought of calling the police flashed through her mind and she almost smiled. That's absurd. It would ruin you before it ruins him. And you know how things work—nothing would come of it. The only thing to do is forget about it. Wipe it out of your mind. Tell yourself it never happened, that it couldn't have happened and it didn't happen. Keep saying it and it'll go away. It didn't happen and it won't ever happen and it wasn't real and you must say it again and again and again: IT DID NOT HAPPEN!

But it was the razor-blade sting of the hot water down there, the blood at her feet—such a deep, pure red against the white of the tub, running so smoothly, so prettily down the drain that it kept her from fooling herself—it was too real and too red to be a lie. But she kept trying, stubbornly against herself, saying it over and over again, until she'd washed her body five times with cool-melon body wash, scrubbing the back of her neck and her ears, then as far around as she could reach over her back, the scent of melon as it lathered, but still not enough to rid the smell of his breath, of coffee, of the sweat and hotness of his tongue in her ear. She tried but couldn't wash herself where it hurt, but when the hot water began to run out it stung less. She washed her body once more before getting out.

Very gently, she dabbed the toilet paper until the bleeding stopped, the bathroom floor wet, the mirror steamed. After she was dressed she slipped a maxi pad into her panties.

She did not go to her next appointment. Instead, she went to King Square and found April and Daisy sitting on one of the benches along the pathway. A swarm of pigeons quivered and pecked at their feet. Daisy flicked a piece of bread, the morsel flying awkwardly from her little fingers as the birds quivered and flapped their wings.

Beyond the square, Prin could see the top floors of the tall building—that building. It didn't happen, she told herself. But she knew he was up there, sitting at his desk, facing the darkened sitting area with the lovely red rug and the panther print and the two—NO—stop. It didn't happen. None of it happened.

"Mommy!" Daisy cried and ran to her. Prin steadied her legs to brace herself but the sudden jolt as Daisy wrapped herself around her waist stung terribly.

"You're early," April said.

Prin forced a smile.

"It's too nice to work today. Besides—" she turned and brushed her hand over Daisy's hair. "I didn't want to miss out on all the fun."

April slid over on the bench.

"Sit."

Prin waved her away.

April stood, and lowered her voice.

"You okay?"

"Fine."

She looked at Prin in disbelief.

"I'm fine, really," Prin said. "Thank you—now go home."

Daisy flicked a piece of bread and the pigeons quivered and swarmed. For a few seconds Prin didn't feel the sting, and she marvelled at how her little girl made everything else in the world disappear. She put out her hand.

"Let's go home."

"Can we stop at the store for a Kinder Egg?" Daisy asked. "I was a good girl for April."

They walked through the square, Daisy dropping breadcrumbs, a parade of pigeons pecking at her heels. Prin walked slowly, in small steps, for Daisy a perfect pace.

When they got home they assembled the tiny toy inside the Kinder Egg; a plastic Tinkerbelle which came in three tinier pieces: head and torso, legs, and wings. Prin lowered herself onto the couch and sighed; not a sigh of defeat, but a sigh of the end of the day, any day, a day like any other, and the relief of it being over. The thought of what happened flashed in her mind and she felt a sting. She grabbed Daisy and strained to lift her up into her lap. Daisy squirmed in her arms, more interested in her new toy.

"Mommy needs a hug," Prin said. "Mommy needs Daisy flowers."

Daisy faced her squarely. There was chocolate on the corners of her mouth.

"It was a beautiful day today, right Mommy?"

Prin stopped herself from crying.

"It was a beautiful day," she said.

"Every day is a beautiful day," Daisy said. She flew the Tinkerbelle and the wings fell off. Prin gathered them from her lap and clicked them on again. She spotted the tulips on the windowsill and a tint of happiness tingled her skin.

"Give Mommy a hug please."

Chapter 3

The black Chrysler 300, with its blacked-out windows, had left Montreal at 9pm, and five hours later was on the outskirts of Edmundston, in the northwest corner of New Brunswick. The tank was empty, the windshield caked in salt. As the car rounded a bend, there, glowing brightly, was an Irving Big Stop nestled into the hillside along a stretch of road which sat perfectly level with the St. John River, which would accompany them all the way to Saint John.

Ivan pulled up to the pump. Dmitri jumped out and hurried inside. Ivan took his time. The crisp air felt good. He stretched and yawned as he filled the tank. Three eighteen-wheelers were parked side by side, nightlights on, the big diesel engines rattling and humming. He grabbed a container of washer fluid from a stack next to the pump, lifted the hood and poured it in. His hands were steady; he didn't spill a drop.

The convenience store's lights were off, as were those in the restaurant at the other end. A plump waitress met him at the diner counter where he paid in cash. The counter was coffee-stained and worn and dirtied along the edges. Three truckers sat, leaning against it; one eating a burger; the other two, sipping on coffee.

Ivan joined Dmitri in a booth in the empty restaurant. The wood-panelled walls were littered with thinly-framed pictures of big-rigs and local minor hockey teams. The waitress flicked on the lights and came with a pot of coffee and filled their cups. Dmitri filled his with sugar.

"Get something to eat," Ivan said.

Dmitri ordered a western sandwich.

"You ever been to Saint John?" he asked.

Ivan shook his head and sipped his coffee.

"I bought a book."

Dmitri grinned.

"A tourist book?"

Ivan nodded.

"Jesus," Dmitri said.

"It has a map," Ivan said.

"Sure," Dmitri said. He sipped his coffee and licked his lips. "So how are we gonna do it? Do we wait until he comes out or go in and get him?"

"Lower your voice," Ivan said.

"Can I decide?" He was licking his lips again.

"Calm down," Ivan said.

"Right—you got the plan—sure."

"You're not a little kid anymore," Ivan said. "This is real. Treat it for what it is." He sipped his coffee. "When Victor put this through I told him you could do this—I told him you were ready. And now you're my responsibility. Don't fuck this up."

Dmitri licked his lips.

A short while later the waitress came with the western sandwich. Dmitri took a big bite, chomping into it. Ivan was right—it was what he needed. He began shovelling the sandwich into his mouth.

"Good?" Ivan asked.

Dmitri nodded, his mouth stuffed full.

"So how does it feel—to really do it?"

"It's a job and you do it," Ivan said.

"But it's gotta feel like something. Sergei says that right before you pull the trigger it feels like fireworks. He says there's nothing like it."

Ivan shook his head.

"Sergei's got a big mouth."

"I bet it feels like something," Dmitri said. "Everything feels like something." He nodded toward the counter, to the truckers. "Let's say we're here to do one of them. How'd we do it?"

"We don't," Ivan said.

Dmitri licked his lips.

"The fat one in the middle—if he's the mark."

"He's not," Ivan said. "Stop being an idiot."

"But let's just say that he is," Dmitri said. "Indulge me."

"Stop it with the tongue," Ivan said.

"Where do we do it—here? Right here in front of everyone? I don't think that'd be good."

"Shut up," Ivan said. He sipped his coffee and waited until Dmitri was calm before he spoke again. "If you act like this when we get to Saint John you'll be waiting in the car."

Dmitri took a deep breath. He couldn't take his eyes off the trucker.

"I'd do it in the parking lot," he said. "Follow him out, get him in the truck and tie him up with the twist ties we got in the trunk. Then I'd slit his throat."

"It's not real—forget about it," Ivan said. "What is real is that we've got another five hours before we get to Saint John." He drank the last of his coffee and signalled to the waitress for more. The waitress came with a fresh pot. "I'll have one of those sandwiches, please." The waitress went into the kitchen and Ivan turned back to Dmitri. "One in the chest, one in the head every time," he said. "Clean and done."

When his sandwich came he took his time eating it, and drank another cup of coffee before calling the waitress over for the bill.

"I gotta take a piss," Dmitri said.

Ivan slid out of the booth.

"I'll be in the car."

He stepped outside and shivered as he walked across the parking lot, past the running rigs to the Chrysler. He and Dmitri had only been in the restaurant for an hour but the car was cold, the seats stiff. The coffee hadn't fully awoken him but the cold did, and he was glad that he was awake now. He started the car, lit a cigarette and sighed to himself. He's not ready, he thought. He's really not ready. But you did this. You took this on. For him. And for you. And you'll see it through.

The lights of the restaurant lit the parking lot. The car was warming. One of the truckers stepped outside. He was as tall as Ivan, but thick like Dmitri, shoulders hunched as he lumbered across the lot, his face tucked into the front of his jacket. Dmitri stepped outside, behind him, the gun in his hand.

Ivan slammed the car into gear and hit the gas, the tires spinning in the snow as it skidded across the lot and slid to a stop alongside Dmitri.

"Get in the car," Ivan said.

The trucker looked back then kept going.

Dmitri climbed in and sunk in his seat.

Ivan steadied his hands on the wheel.

"You do something like that and Victor finds out and we're both dead."

"I wasn't really gonna do it," Dmitri said.

Ivan lit another cigarette.

"Get some sleep."

Chapter 4

The lights were dim in the Bourbon Quarter. A small crowd had gathered at the tables near the bar that ran the length of the old brick wall. There was a microphone set up at the front, and in the window facing Prince William Street was a poster that said OPEN MIC POETRY TONIGHT 9-11PM.

Charlie was sitting in a booth with the owner, Shawn Verner, and he looked down at his papers, of the few poems he'd written in the last week. Shawn refilled their glasses, emptying the pitcher of beer.

"How'd your date go last night?"

Charlie huffed, half smiling, a handsome, boyish glint in his eye, betrayed only by the thinning hairline, the grey of his whiskers.

"No offense, but that's the last time your wife sets me up."

"That bad, eh?"

"We got talking about books," Charlie said. "Then she said: Would you believe me if I told you I've never read anything other than Harlequin Romance? To which I replied: Yes. It pretty much went downhill from there."

"Not everyone's into Bukowski," Shawn said. He was plump in the cheeks and his chin doubled when he smiled.

"Does Jess read Harlequin Romance?" Charlie asked.

Shawn smiled again.

"I couldn't do it," Charlie said. "Sorry."

Shawn stepped over to the bar and returned with another pitcher of beer. An older woman got up to the mic and started to read from a wire-ringed notebook. She had a nose ring, her hair dishevelled; a look of wildness, but when she opened her mouth she was monotone; plain, and quite unlike what Charlie had expected.

"Jesus, she reads like Atwood," he said. "Have you ever seen Atwood read?"

"No," Shawn said.

"She's like a robot. The only thing that saves her are the words." He listened for a moment to the woman at the mic. "But she doesn't have it. But who does these days?"

"So listen," Shawn said. "Jessica's pregnant again."

Charlie held up his glass.

"Congrats, man."

"We want you to be the godfather."

"Me?"

"Yeah you."

"And Jessica's okay with this?"

"It was her idea. She sees how good you are with Claire."

Charlie was nodding.

"Thanks, man—that'd be real nice."

They clinked their glasses. Then there was a brief but awkward moment when neither spoke, and though Charlie and Shawn had been friends since high school it was a noticeable silence.

"The right girl's out there," Shawn said.

Charlie smiled.

"I know. I found her once. I'll find her again."

Shawn sighed.

"Who, the hooker? You gotta give that up."

"She wasn't a hooker."

"No?"

"It wasn't like that," Charlie said. "She wasn't like that with me."

"But you paid her."

"Not for the whole weekend."

"She gave you a discount," Shawn said. "That's love, I guess."

"She didn't read Harlequin Romances," Charlie said.

The next day the air was crisp and the sky blue. Charlie had eaten his lunch in his car, a rusted Volkswagen Golf with a CANADA POST decal on the side. A pint of Canadian Club sat on the seat, a six-pack of Alpine on the floor. He was parked at the end of the wharf at the Rothesay Yacht Club, the marina now empty in the winter. Across the Kennebecasis River was a sheer rock face and the hills and trees on Kingston Peninsula. To his right he could see a few of the big old houses overlooking the river.

Charlie balled up the tinfoil wrap from his sandwich and gulped down a beer. His plan each day was to work fast so he'd finish the first part of his route by noon—the bungalows and side-splits in Quispamsis—so he could relax in the afternoon and enjoy his route along Rothesay Road with its tall trees that cast a mess of shadows onto the road and the Victorian mansions along the river. It was fun to imagine that he lived in one of those big houses; that his life really was as splendid and as perfect as those who lived there.

His favourite house sat far off the road, hidden by a wall of high cedars. A shaded veranda wrapped around the front, bare in the winter. But in the summer there were wicker chairs and flower pots hanging and swaying in the breeze. This is where Charlie imagined he'd sit and drink wine. He grinned at the thought of it. A nice bottle of cabernet, he thought. Something expensive, something reviewed in a magazine that described it as going down like silk. Shit, yes, he thought. What a life. He was still thinking of the wine as he climbed out of his car with the two envelopes in hand, the hard-crusted snow breaking under his feet.

The steps to the veranda hadn't been shovelled and there were rolled up newspapers against the doorway, the mailbox filled with letters and bills he'd already delivered. He leaned against the door and peeked through one of the windows. The house was still.

He walked around the veranda, to the side of the house. He cupped his hands and pressed his face against the window and looked inside. There were big cushioned chairs, a leather sofa, and two bookshelves on each side of a fireplace. He squinted to look further, his face pressed against the window, and he felt the window move. It was unlocked. Whether it was the beer he'd had for lunch, or the thought of actually seeing his favorite house up close, for whatever reason, he was compelled to continue. He slid his fingers under the windowpane, slid it open, and poked his head inside. He'd only ever been as far as the front entrance, and only in the wintertime when Mrs. Staal would invite him in, out of the cold, while she fetched her purse for her credit card to pay for god-knows-what she'd bought online that week. Just the smell of the house made his mind wander, thinking that yes, if he were a doctor he would have a house like this—or a big-name writer, he thought. He wanted to sit in one of those cushioned chairs—just to see what it felt like. He leaned on the windowsill and lifted his leg and stepped inside—stepped into it, into this new and wonderful place.

The room was brighter than what it looked from outside, with the sunlight coming through the long windows. I could write a novel in this room, Charlie thought. He went into the kitchen, where it was very bright, a table and chairs under a solarium looking out to a small garage and a snow-covered garden that couldn't be seen from the front of the house. Charlie recognized the foyer where he'd stood many times before. It felt odd seeing it from this angle. From where he stood the front door and the side window were perfectly framed by the hallway and he wondered if he'd looked like a painting or a photograph those times he'd stood there, and if Mrs. Staal had seen it that way too. I doubt it, he thought.

Two hours later he found himself back in the city, parked on the curb in front of his building. The empty pint of whiskey sat on the seat beside him, the empty beer cans on the floor. He didn't want to go inside, where the stairs were narrow and there was litter in the hall, where his apartment smelled musty and unkempt and was very small and had a cheap bookshelf and a sink filled with dishes. And there was laundry to do—he'd put it in a garbage bag and left it by the door on his way to work so he wouldn't forget it. But now he remembered it and the thought of going to the Laundromat depressed him. He thought of his poems but the dinginess of his building depressed him, and he knew he wasn't Bukowski—his life didn't inspire him this way. He knew his writing wasn't important and never would be, and he wondered why he ever went to open mic night. He wondered if the people there thought his poetry was as pathetic as he now felt it was, sitting in his car drinking, feeling sorry for himself, feeling small and unnecessary and guilty of something—he didn't know of what, maybe his life—the way it had turned out. Get out of the car and get inside, he thought. Face it and forget it—it's life, my life, and that's that.

He smelled weed as soon as he stepped into his building and right away it brought a feeling of hope—that the night still wasn't over—and so he climbed the extra flight of stairs to Jeremy Wiggins' apartment and knocked on the door. Nobody answered. He knocked again, this time harder.

"I know you're in there," he said.

Jeremy answered the door.

"What's going on?" Charlie said. He was happy again, smelling the weed. "Is this a bad time?"

"Just dealing with a little problem," Jeremy said. "Come on in."

When Jeremy Wiggins arrived home from work earlier that evening he'd smelled the weed in the staircase. He was tired, and there was nothing more pleasing after a long day than going home and smoking a joint and relaxing on the couch. And so he liked smelling the weed, thinking it was coming from Charlie's apartment, but once he got to the third floor he realized it was coming from his own. He opened the door and there was Eddie Smythe, sitting on his couch. Eddie sprung up and offered him the joint.

"I tried calling you, man. You didn't answer your phone."

Jeremy sighed.

"I haven't stopped all day." He looked like a young Bob Dylan with his black and white suit and thin black tie, his head of messy curls, his long nose and thin lips. "My parents are away so it's just me and Carol running things." He loosened his tie and took the joint. "What's going on?"

"Not much," Eddie said.

Eddie had never been to Jeremy's apartment this early in the day before. Just once, Jeremy thought, and that was because I shorted him by mistake and he wanted his money. He handed the joint back to Eddie and stepped over the cord that ran from the TV to the coffee table where a Sony Xbox and two controllers sat amongst dirty glasses, an old newspaper, an ashtray with overflowing cigarette butts, and a wooden cigar box, opened, containing a block of hash, a bag of weed, and a pack of rolling papers. Jeremy noticed the cleared space at the end of the table and the baggie of cocaine.

Eddie handed the joint back.

"I need a place to crash for a few days."

"What's wrong with your place?" Jeremy said.

Eddie shrugged.

"You in trouble or something?" Jeremy asked.

"Everything's cool, man."

"What'd you do?"

"Nothing."

"The cops looking for you?"

"No."

Jeremy sighed.

"Cut the bullshit."

Eddie cut a couple lines of coke with his bank card, snorted a line then sat up. He was lanky with a thin face, and when he sat up his eyes bulged. He nodded, half to himself.

"They're gonna kill me."

"Who?"

"The Ukrainians. The mafia."

"The real mafia?"

"The real deal," Eddie said.

"What for?"

"I owe them."

"How much?"

"Twelve grand."

"Jesus!" Jeremy said. "How'd that happen?"

Eddie snorted another line and popped his head back up.

"No idea, man."

Jeremy gave him the joint.

Eddie took a long haul.

"The boss, Victor, called me last night—said he was calling to say goodbye."

Jeremy went to the kitchen, opened the fridge, poured some juice and stood with the fridge door open. He took a long drink then refilled his glass and sat down on the couch.

Eddie lit a cigarette, his hand shaking, the joint in one hand, the cigarette in the other.

Then came a knock at the door.

They froze, wide-eyed.

Another knock, this time louder.

"I know you're in there," the voice said.

"Relax," Jeremy said. "It's just Charlie from downstairs."

He opened the door.

"What's going on?" Charlie grinned. "Is this a bad time?"

"Just dealing with a little problem," Jeremy said. "Come on in."

Charlie sat in the armchair adjacent to the couch. He'd never met Eddie before and so he simply nodded. Jeremy introduced Charlie and then explained to him the trouble Eddie was in.

"I don't know what to tell you," Charlie said. He noticed the coke on the table. "I just came here to smoke a joint."

Eddie started rolling another joint.

"You could change your name," Charlie said. "Go out west and get a job in the oil fields—there's real money out there."

"Henry James," Eddie said, focused on the joint. "I'd change my name to Henry James."

"Like the writer?" Charlie said.

Eddie shrugged.

"Never heard of him—just like the sound of it." He lit the joint and took a haul then passed it to Charlie.

"When are they coming?" Charlie asked.

"They're probably already on their way," Eddie said.

"Are you safe here?"

"Sure, man."

"Then why don't you just lie low here?"

Jeremy stepped in and took the joint from Charlie.

"This is a small city—they'd find him in no time. They'd ask a neighbour if Eddie has any friends and the neighbour says sure, man, he's always got people over. Then they go and find one person who knows my name and we're both dead."

Charlie slunk back in the chair.

"So what you're saying is that these guys are coming here—to this apartment—no matter what."

Jeremy perked up.

"Jesus, I never thought of that."

Eddie took the joint from Jeremy.

"I'll catch the Greyhound first thing in the morning."

Jeremy's arms waved about.

"WHAT HAVE YOU GOTTEN ME INTO?"

Eddie put up his hands.

"Calm down, bro."

"I'm not your bro, man."

"That's harsh, dude."

"HARSH? YOU'VE SENT THIS TO MY FRONT DOOR!"

"You can hide out at my place," Charlie said. "Both of you. It's just me there."

"We need a plan," Eddie said.

Charlie crossed his arms.

"You've got two choices, fight or flee."

"He's no gangsta," Jeremy said, nodding at Eddie. "He may think he is because he listens to Snoop Dogg, but deep down he's Justin Bieber."

"Who's being harsh now?" Eddie said.

Jeremy sighed.

"This is too fucked up. I can't believe this is happening." He went to the kitchen for another glass of juice and drank it down. "We can't stay here—we know that much. We can maybe crash at the funeral home till my parents get back—that'll buy us a few days."

"Sleep in a coffin," Eddie said.

"Yeah," Jeremy said. "Keep joking about it, man. Meanwhile, we're both dead, thanks to you."

Chapter 5

Walter Stephens sat in the chair between the two big windows at Wiggins Funeral Home. He looked over at the casket. From where he sat he could see his nephew's face, glowing under the lights. It's all your fault, he thought. A thud of guilt dropped into his gut. He could see the portrait he'd just placed on Eddie's chest and he looked around the empty room and thought of his sister, Iris—Eddie's mother. Her wake was packed, he thought. He couldn't remember if it was in this same room; it had felt so much smaller with so many people. But here the room was open, empty.

Iris and her husband were killed in a car accident in 1993. They'd gone to Fredericton to see an exhibit at the art gallery and were on their way home. It had been a beautiful fall day with all the colors in the waves of hills through Oromocto, Gagetown, and Welsford. The police report stated that at that particular hour, approximately 5:30pm, and on that stretch of highway, the setting sun would have shone directly into drivers' eyes. The report also stated that there were no skid marks at the scene. They never saw the moose at all.

Things had moved very quickly and formally for Walter; it seemed everyone spoke with papers in hand, rehearsed and prepared, the polar opposite of how he was feeling, the suddenness of his sister's death, how suddenly she'd been plucked from life. There'd been the lawyer who spoke in short form, as though he'd prepared and referred to cheat sheets and all he said were the most important parts. *The house still has a mortgage. You'll have to sell.* There was the social worker, who kept looking down at her notes. *The boy is legally yours. Have you found a school for him? You'll have to do that. You should go to the house and get some of his things—toys, blankets—things familiar to him.* Walter went that afternoon. He'd never been in Iris's house alone. He'd felt like an intruder. The stillness of the house, the quietness of it told him she was really gone. All of her belongings, the furniture, dishes, pictures; all these things were just things now, objects that belonged to another time. He filled two suitcases with toys; Star Wars and GI Joe figurines, dinky cars, and Lego, and two garbage bags with clothes and blankets—Teenage Mutant Ninja Turtles sheets and pillowcases. On his way out he passed, in the front hallway, a portrait of Iris. He'd always loved this picture, in black and white, taken at her graduation from UNB. The sun was on her face, on her freckles, and there was sunlight in her hair. She was squinting and smiling slightly, as if she knew something nobody else did. Walter removed it from the wall, brought it home and hung it above his dresser.

Walter turned from the casket and looked out the window, over the highway, to the lights of the Harbour Bridge, and another thud dropped into his gut, not one of guilt, but of gloom. He'd worked the tolls since 1979 and today had been his last day. At 4pm the tolls were no more. For years the bridge had been a debt to the city; the constant upkeep was costing millions in loans and the city had finally convinced the federal government to wipe out the debt and rid the residents of the tolls.

He turned again and peered over at the portrait on Eddie's chest, of the glow of the casket at the far end of the room. This was the room Iris was in, he thought. And it was the same size then as it is now. The same goddamned room.

After Eddie had moved in so many years ago there'd been a tinge of hope in Walter's life; that the prospect of his young nephew coming to live with him might be something good, something to look forward to. But it wasn't that way. The instant connection Walter was hoping for with Eddie never came, and very soon afterwards he realized what a burden raising this boy would be. But despite his feelings, he had every intention of raising his sister's child as she would have wanted—with love and caring—even if these things required a conscious effort.

That first night in the apartment Walter had gone out and gotten McDonalds' for dinner. They sat on the floor, eating at the coffee table.

"So," he finally said, swallowing the last of his Big Mac. "What do you want to do tonight?"

Eddie shrugged and picked at his fries.

"Do you want to play checkers?" Walter asked.

Eddie shook his head.

"There must be something you like to play," Walter said.

"Hide and seek," Eddie muttered.

Walter perked up.

"I can do that. Do you want to hide first?"

"You hide," Eddie said.

Walter stood up. Eddie closed his eyes and counted to ten. When he opened his eyes Walter had vanished. Eddie went into the bedroom and looked under the bed, then into Walter's room, to the closet, then the kitchen, the bathroom. Walter was nowhere to be found.

"Okay, I give up," Eddie said.

"I'm right here," Walter said. He'd been standing right beside the lamp along the wall. Eddie had walked by him twice.

"How'd you do that?" he said.

Walter was grinning.

They played hide and seek every night for a month, and each time Walter managed to find the most obvious places to hide without being found; behind the curtains, beside the fridge, next to the coat rack by the front door. It was a good first month, and Walter was beginning to think that his first impressions of life with Eddie were wrong. But then, a week later, Eddie head-butted a boy at school and was suspended for a day. A year later he pushed a boy off the monkey bars, breaking the boy's arm in the fall. He was suspended for three days. Walter hadn't said anything when he had to take those days off work without pay to stay at home. When Eddie was thirteen he came home drunk for the first time. He'd sat on the couch, swaying and staring blankly across the room.

"It's not good for you—being this young," Walter had said. "You could choke on your own vomit—and then you'd be done! What do you think about that?"

Eddie giggled and swayed.

"I'm going to bed."

"Good then," Walter said.

And Eddie went to bed and that was that.

Soon Eddie started staying out all night and Walter did not know what to do, and so he did nothing but wait for him to get home in the morning.

"You can't be out all night—not all night—by god, something could happen to you!"

And Eddie would go to bed again.

It was around this time that something happened; something strange and wonderful and frightening, and it changed Walter's life forever.

A voice had awoken him in the middle of the night.

Walter, it had said.

Walter wasn't sure if he was awake or dreaming.

He sat up in bed.

"Eddie, is that you?"

He listened.

Walter, it said again.

Walter squinted, trying to adjust his eyes to the darkness.

A car passed, its lights swooning across the bedroom wall.

You're dreaming, he thought. Go back to sleep. He lay back down and closed his eyes. When he awoke in the morning he figured it had been a dream; nothing but a vivid dream.

But the next night, the voice awoke him again.

Walter.

Walter shot up and sat as still as he could. I'm not going crazy, he thought. I'm not going to lie back down and hear it again—not again. He remained upright, until his eyes adjusted a little to the darkness, to the silhouette of his dresser and the strangely faded yellow wallpaper and its sprawling flamboyant patterns.

Walter.

Walter sprung from his bed and turned on the bedroom light. It was a sudden hard light and it stung his eyes. He turned to the portrait of Iris above the dresser.

Walter, it said.

Walter's heart beat fast in his chest. It was the portrait. It was Iris. There was no mistaking it. He plucked it from off the wall. It was that smile, that mischievous, slight smile.

I'm here, Iris said.

Walter gasped.

"Is this happening? This isn't happening. Is it? It isn't. It's not you, not really. Is it?"

Of course it's me, Iris said.

"But how?"

Don't think of that.

Walter's mind raced, searching for a way to rationalize it, to justify it to himself. Then the small wooden crucifix on the wall next to the closet caught his eye. It had been there since he'd moved in back in 1985; his apartment had come fully furnished and over the years he'd replaced just about everything, but the crucifix had remained. Walter had never given religion much thought, and he'd left the crucifix where it was and over the years he'd almost forgotten it was there; he'd gotten so used to it that he didn't notice it anymore. Until now.

"Are you God?" he asked the portrait.

Don't be silly, Iris said.

"Then you're just like God," he said. "Lots of people believe in

God and they aren't crazy, so why would I be crazy to believe in you? Would I be any different than anyone else?"

Of course not, Iris said.

Walter glanced toward the door, toward Eddie's room.

"I don't know where he is. I never know where he is anymore."

You're doing fine, Iris said. Now go back to sleep.

As Walter sat by the window he now felt somewhere in between it all; in between his dead nephew and the bridge. An anxiousness settled over him. He wanted to go home to his apartment with its warm, stale air which smelled of his musty old couch, of the worn carpet and his Colt cigars. There he knew he belonged; he'd always have a place there. Here the room was empty, as empty as he imagined Eddie's life had been. As empty as your own, he thought, looking over to the casket, to the portrait on his Eddie's chest. His own voice even felt empty to him now.

Chapter 6

Prin awoke early. Sunlight shone through her bedroom window, through the curtains that swayed in the heat of the coil radiator. She crept into the kitchen and made a cup of tea. She liked the feeling of being inside and warm, knowing it was cold outside. And she liked the quiet, the creaks the kitchen floor made under her feet. She'd almost forgotten what had happened to her, until she sat at the table and the pain shrieked inside her and she hopped off the chair. And with that, she went into the living room with her tea.

She sat carefully on the couch and tried to find that pleasant feeling the sun had given her. She looked outside. The building across the street had frost on the windows. She sipped her tea. You always take your morning tea in the kitchen, she thought. She got up gingerly and tiptoed across the floor, to the kitchen, trying again to sit in the chair, denying the pain as it shot up her, through her, her eyes watering until her buttocks were flat on the chair and she gripped the kitchen table, held on for a few seconds and let her body settle into it. She sipped again. It didn't happen, she thought. Tell yourself this a thousand times and you'll believe it. You can make what's real not real by denying it, by not believing in it so that it disappears. Her mind relaxed in the stillness of the kitchen, in the bright patch of sunlight on the floor and the specks of dust floating in the light.

Daisy came into the kitchen, stepping into the patch of light. Her eyes were puffy, a tuft of hair on top of her head. She stretched her arms and yawned.

Prin smiled.

"It's early, Pumpkin-head—you can go back to sleep if you want." She lifted herself from the chair and winced. "But I suppose you want breakfast?"

Daisy climbed up onto a chair, her chin level with the edge of the table. "Pancakes."

"But you had them yesterday—you sure you want them again?"

"Yup."

"How about eggs?"

"Pancakes," Daisy said.

"What do you say?"

"Please!"

Prin grinned and fetched a big glass bowl and the box of pancake mix from the cupboard.

"You're going to turn into a pancake you eat them so much. What would Mommy do if Daisy turned into a pancake?"

Daisy laughed at this.

"You're silly, Mommy!"

Prin got the fry pan out, turned on the stove and poured the batter. Then the phone rang. It was April. She was worried about Prin, that she knew she was lying to her yesterday and when she went home she couldn't stop thinking about it.

"You're a dear friend," Prin said. She flipped the pancake, her head tilted to her shoulder to hold the phone. "I'm fine—really. But thank you."

April said she knew she was lying but she wouldn't press her about it, and that Prin could call her anytime if she ever needed to talk. "I don't know how you do it," she said.

"It's not for everyone," Prin said.

"Well if you're interested, there's a flyer at the Laundromat for the tour guide course. I know you've always wanted to do that."

"For what, ten dollars an hour?"

"Okay, okay, I won't say anything else," April said.

Prin scooped the first pancake onto a plate and placed it on the table in front of Daisy. She grabbed the bottle of maple syrup but it was empty and so she plucked a jar of honey, untwisted the lid and poured it on. She turned back to the fry pan, facing the stove, when Daisy started spitting her pancake onto the plate.

"Yucky!"

"What's wrong?"

Daisy scraped her tongue with her fork.

"This syrup is yucky, Mommy!"

Prin turned back to the stove, to the butter burning in the pan.

"April, I've got to let you go—" She hung up and turned back to Daisy. "Mommy will get some more syrup later, but for now this is all we've got."

Daisy was sticking out her tongue.

"It's yucky!"

"Oh hush," Prin said.

They watched TV all day and played with Daisy's dolls, then ordered pizza for supper. At six o'clock they headed to the Laundromat. Prin was feeling better. The pain had subsided and she could move around almost normally. It didn't hurt as she carried the clothes basket, Daisy skipping alongside her on the sidewalk. The night was cold and still, the sky, which had been so blue all day, was now black. They turned the corner onto Princess Street. The warm light of the Laundromat lit the sidewalk. Prin loved the Laundromat. She loved the smell of fabric softener, the hum of the washers, the spinning of the dryers, the green-tiled floor and the whiteness of all the machines. She loved the brightness and the moist, sauna-like heat that steamed up the big front window with the cold winter night outside. Daisy sat on the floor and played with her dolls.

"This one is my favourite," she said, holding up a tiny pink dress she'd just stripped from a doll.

"I like it too," Prin said. "Is it Lady Buttercup's?"

"Lady Buttercup gave it to Princess Fiona."

"That was nice of her."

"She didn't want it anymore."

"Well it was still nice of her to share," Prin said.

She dropped the lid and placed the quarters into the slot, started up the machine, then sat in one of the chairs by the front window. And there it was, on a plain white piece of paper tacked to the wall:

CITY TOUR GUIDES WANTED

NIGHT COURSE RUNS TUESDAY APRIL 5TH AND WEDNESDAY APRIL 7TH IN THE BASEMENT AT THE CATHEDRAL OF THE IMMACULATE CONCEPTION, 91 WATERLOO STREET, 7PM. $80 FOR BOTH NIGHTS. REGISTRATION FIRST COME FIRST SERVED.

Ten dollars an hour, she thought.

She bent low and lifted up Daisy and plopped her onto the chair beside her. She felt the chill from the big window as she looked outside. Wires crisscrossed the street. A car drove slowly by, its exhaust smoking in the cold, the driver bundled up and close to the wheel. Then Daisy dropped one of her dolls, and as Prin bent down to pick it up a man came in, the cold air whooshing in behind him. She knew who it was the instant she looked up—she knew it was Charlie. Then Charlie glanced over at her and their eyes met, and Charlie smiled, and Prin's heart fluttered. She stood up and took a step toward him.

"Hello, Charles."

Charlie recognized her right away. He remembered how she'd called him Charles and not Charlie, and how it had refined her in some small way; it was one of the things that had drawn him to her.

"How long has it been?" he asked.

"A while," she said.

He looked down at Daisy.

"Yours?"

Prin smiled and nodded.

"And now you're a mom," Charlie said. He rolled on the balls of his feet. "She's some cute."

Prin smiled again.

"What's her name?" Charlie asked.

"Daisy."

"Like the flower? I remember you liked those."

Prin nodded again. She was still smiling.

"I haven't seen you around," Charlie said.

"I don't do the bar scene anymore."

"Well that's good," Charlie said. "It's good to be done with all of that."

The corners of Prin's mouth dropped a little, but not enough for Charlie to notice.

"So what are you doing then—just being a mom, I suppose?" He watched as Daisy climbed off the chair and sat on the floor and played with her dolls.

"She's very bright," Prin said. "She loves books—she loves to read."

"Did you ever read those books I gave you?" Charlie asked.

"Some of them—I don't have much time to read."

"No, I guess not."

"I still have them," Prin quickly said. "I'll get them back to you."

"No, no—they were for you to keep. Maybe Daisy would like to read them someday."

"I think she might."

A washing machine buzzed.

They stood, silent, looking at each other.

"She's yours, Charles."

Charlie didn't say anything.

"I wanted to tell you sooner," Prin said.

Charlie was nodding, a bit dazed.

"How do you know?"
"I use protection with everyone."
"But you didn't with me," Charlie said.
"That wasn't work," Prin said. "Not for me."
Charlie was still nodding, still a bit dazed.
"I'm no good with these kinds of things, Prin."
"I never asked if you were."
"I don't have any money."
"I never asked if you did. We're doing fine."
There was another silent moment between them.
"Why didn't you tell me?" Charlie said.
"I didn't know how."
"You could have just told me."
"I couldn't find you," Prin said. "And I was afraid."
"Afraid of what?"
Prin's eyes started to water.
"I don't know. It was a crazy time."
"So what about the last five years?"
Prin started to cry.
Charlie took a step back.
"I'm sorry," he said. "It's a lot to take in. Does she know?"
"No."
Charlie looked down again at the little girl who was playing with her doll.
"Shit, she's some cute."
"I don't want anything from you, Charles."
Charlie scratched the back of his head and took a step back. "Holy shit. It really is a lot to take in. I just came here to wash my clothes." He didn't know what else to say. "It's pretty cold out there tonight." He turned and started back toward the dryers. "Let's get together for coffee or something."
"I'd like that," Prin said.
Charlie stuffed the rest of his clothes into the garbage bag then

walked back to the front where Prin was sitting by the window again. Daisy was sitting in her lap, looking down, focused on her doll.

"It was good seeing you, Prin."

"You too, Charles."

Charlie looked down at Daisy and smiled. And with that, he stepped out into the cold. That beautiful little girl, he thought. How did that happen? But he knew. That afternoon up on the roof. The beer and the boats far out in the bay and the sun sparkling off the water, and the sky so blue it didn't even look real.

He walked along the salt-covered sidewalk.

Maybe you've known all along, he thought. Prin was always in the back of your mind, ever since that day. He remembered times in the bars when he thought he'd seen her in the crowd. She was always there, he thought. Everywhere but nowhere, and now there she is, with a little girl that's yours and it's all right in front of you, all together and all at once. You couldn't have dreamed it up any better. He felt the warmth of his clothes through the garbage bag. And by god she's as lovely as she was before, only older, wiser—and more confident. She's become the woman you'd imagined and there she is, her and the little girl, and whatever you do don't fuck it up—don't go and fuck it up so she leaves again.

He raced back to the Laundromat and stopped before going inside; he could see her by the window in that warm yellow light, and the little girl—his daughter—in her lap.

Prin stood up when he walked in.

Charlie plopped the garbage bag on the floor and took a moment to catch his breath.

"After our weekend together I went for two months watching you every night when you came home."

Prin frowned.

"You were stalking me?"

"No, it wasn't like that—"

"You were watching me come home every night?"

Charlie looked down at the floor.

"Okay, it was like that. But it wasn't in a weird stalker way or anything—I just wanted to make sure you were okay each night—that you got home safe."

"I'm a big girl."

"I know that."

"But thank you, Charles."

Daisy held up her doll to Prin, and Prin smiled.

"Then all of a sudden you weren't there anymore," Charlie said. "You just vanished."

"I moved to Millidgeville. I didn't want to be uptown."

"But you moved back."

"Of course. This is my home."

Charlie grinned, his breathing back to normal.

"I'm writing again. I've got a poetry collection I'm putting together to shop around. I go to the Bourbon Quarter and read at open mic night. I could read some to you—they might be a bit much for Daisy but I could some write nursery rhymes if I tried. Maybe she could come over and I could read to her and I could make up the small bedroom and fill it with toys and maybe she could come over if it's okay with you—maybe you could come over together."

Prin was smiling.

"Slow down, Charles. I only came here to wash clothes too."

"Sorry," he said. "This is all surreal to me—to have you standing here in front of me. And her—" He looked down at Daisy. "Where do we start?"

"I don't know," Prin said.

"Forget coffee—how about lunch, tomorrow."

"Okay," Prin said. "But I think it's better if it's just me and you. I'll call April."

"I remember her—she cut your hair," Charlie said. "I see you've still got it short—not as long as it once was."

"Not as short as when April first cut it."

"No, that was very short."

"But I liked it very short."

"I did too," Charlie said. "Do you think you'd ever cut it that short again?"

"Let's not talk about it or we'll have nothing to talk about tomorrow."

Chapter 7

Charlie woke up the next morning, called in sick for work then skipped over to the convenience store and bought a coffee and a newspaper. It was a grey day. He walked the few blocks to Eddie's apartment and climbed the stairs. He couldn't believe he'd agreed to do this; that he'd gotten involved with this whole mess with Jeremy and Eddie. What a ridiculous thing to be doing for nothing; risking his own life simply because he was high and thought, sure, why not? He sat on the floor with his back against the wall. He could hear the door downstairs whenever it opened, and every time it opened his heart jumped. He tried to take his mind off of things by reading the newspaper. The absurdity of the newspaper. The front page had pictures of the toll bridge and there were articles on the history of the bridge and the closing of the tolls.

He pulled out his pen and wrote a quick poem on the back of the paper. It wasn't any good and he knew it, and there came that feeling of hopelessness when he wanted to write a good poem but knew it just wasn't the right time for it. He wondered how long he might have to wait for the killer to arrive. Or was there more than one? Eddie said there would likely be two. But how would he know that? And how serious was all of this? Was it even real? Eddie struck him as a bit of a moron. What if nobody came? Even better, he thought. I can go home and get on with my day—and my life. His stomach rumbled at the thought of seeing Prin again. And his daughter. Jesus. Then his stomach rumbled again, but not with anxiousness, but because he had to shit. Put it out of your mind, he told himself. Don't think of it and you won't have to go. But it didn't work. It never works, he thought. It's the one thing you can't wish away for very long. He stood up and tried Eddie's door and it opened. He scampered across the room and into the bathroom.

Splotches of dried toothpaste lined the sink. The tub was stained yellow. Charlie sat, trying to rationalize everything in his head. He was a father. He had no idea what that meant. His stomach swirled and he couldn't tell if it was a good feeling or not—it scared him more than what he was doing now.

Then he heard the apartment door open and the footsteps that followed.

They were here, and they were real. He froze, unable to move, as though he'd been turned to stone. He thought of Dostoevsky's *Crime and Punishment*. You're Raskolnikov behind the door, he thought. He could feel his heart racing. He took a deep breath then stood from the toilet, and as he did, his hand knocked a cup into the sink and it clanked and clattered before he snatched it up. He pulled up his pants and waited, still as a statue.

Ivan had smoked nearly a whole pack of cigarettes in the remaining five hours to Saint John while Dmitri had slept. There was a dry, stale heat in the car and he cracked the window for some fresh air, then lit another cigarette. Dmitri awoke as they slowed at the tolls and crossed the bridge. He looked over the railing, to the city at the edge of the water; the brown and red of the old brick buildings on the hillside, the patina green of church steeples and the smoke of chimneys rising into the grey-black morning sky.

"Find the address on the map," Ivan said.

Dmitri rubbed the sleep from his eyes then grabbed Ivan's book from the glove box. "Take the first right once you get off the bridge." He looked again out over the railing. "I'm hungry."

"We'll eat after," Ivan said.

"Can we get a coffee?—I need a coffee."

"No," Ivan said. He turned off at Main Street and followed it uptown, past the Aquatic Centre and into the heart of the city, at water level, by Market Square. He veered right, onto Water Street where the old buildings carved out a piece of the land along the street at the water's edge. Ivan drove slowly, looking at the Victorian brickwork, the tall arched windows, and despite the dreariness of the day he knew how lovely it all looked, the old buildings on the hillside and the churches with their green steeples; this was a city time had touched with both humility and beauty and he felt it as he drove.

Water Street turned into Lower Cove Loop and worked its way around the harbour, past the port with its long blue warehouse with the paint chipping away in the salt air. The huge parking lot was filled with cars. Yellow Sunbury rigs were backed into the building. The cranes at the port were bright yellow, more yellow than the rigs, especially with the low sky.

Dmitri felt it too, the greyness of it all, but then he realized how close he was, how he'd waited so long for this and now it was about to happen. He rubbed his palms on his thighs then checked the map again.

"We should be looking for Carmarthen Street, coming up on the left."

Ivan flicked his cigarette out the window and turned onto Carmarthen.

"What number?"

"155."

The car crept along until they found the building; a small, pastel blue three-story walk-up. Ivan parked along the street, a half block away. Dmitri reached into the glove box and handed Ivan his gun—a small semi-automatic pistol—and silencer. Ivan held it low, screwed on the silencer and cocked it and slipped it in his jacket pocket. Dmitri was holding his gun now too—the silencer already on.

"Stay focused," Ivan said.

Dmitri licked his lips.

"Stop it with the lips," Ivan said.

They climbed out of the car and entered the building. There were mailboxes in the small entry and there it was, **E. SMYTHE—apt 3C**. They climbed the stairs, guns at their sides.

The door was open. They stepped inside.

Shadows moved under the bathroom door. Charlie was frozen, his hand still gripping the cup that had fallen into the sink. He was still thinking of Dostoevsky. Follow the plan, he thought. It's the only way out of this. In a flash he envisioned what he was going to do and how he was going to do it. He breathed again and stepped into the hall.

Five minutes later, Ivan and Dmitri were back in the car. Ivan unscrewed the silencer from his gun and placed it in the glove box, lit a cigarette and dropped the book into Dmitri's lap.

"Find us a place to eat."

"I don't care," Dmitri groaned.

"Listen to me, what's done is done."

Dmitri shook his head. He opened the book and directed Ivan downtown where they parked near the water and walked up the steep ascent of Germain Street. Dmitri, with the book in his hand, pointed to Reggie's Restaurant.

They sat at a table along the wall nearest to the front window. The place was bustling with customers, the murmurs of morning conversations, cutlery clinking on plates, the sliding of chairs. On the wall above them was a world map with tacks all over it. The waitress came over with two menus.

"Two coffees to start," Ivan said. "And a tack for your map." There was the smell of morning, of city workers, of coffee and bacon and toast and jam. "We've got the whole day to kill," he said. "Let's try to enjoy it."

Dmitri was slumped in his chair.

"What was your first one like?"

Ivan cleared his throat.

"I don't talk about those things." When the tack came he stuck it on Kiev, sat back down and sipped his coffee. "Victor needs things that need done. I'll make the call tonight and he checks it off and moves on. He doesn't care about who did what or how it was done—only that it was done, and done clean. Next time another job comes up you'll get another shot. I know you're disappointed—I know that—but these things happen."

"Sergei says there's nothing like it."

Ivan huffed.

"Stop listening to Sergei." He flipped through the book. "Let's do something. We're not sitting in the car all day. There's some nice architecture here."

Dmitri frowned.

"Since when do you care about that shit?" Outside the window it was starting to snow. "I don't care what we do as long as I stay warm."

Chapter 8

When Lee Peters was arrested he was dressed in a puffy winter jacket, baggy pants, basketball shoes and a Lakers cap he wore sideways. Detective John Ladd had let Peters sit in the interrogation room for an hour, watching him stew in his chair before entering and dropping the file on the table. He offered Peters a cigarette, which he accepted, then opened the file.

"This isn't good, Lee—selling to an undercover. With your priors this isn't going to look good to the judge."

Peters smoked. He didn't like Detective Ladd, with his bright red hair, like Archie.

Ladd sat back and crossed his arms.

"It would go a long way if you helped us out—tell us what you know."

"I don't know shit," Peters said.

"Who's your supplier?"

"I found it in the club."

"All six baggies, or just the one you sold to the officer?"

Peters scoffed.

Ladd leaned over the table.

"How many times have you been in here?"

Peters scoffed again and smoked.

"This can go one of two ways, Lee," Ladd said. "You can cooperate and things look a whole lot better. Or you can sit here and play it cool and take it to the judge. And let me tell you, it isn't going to be some weekend stint—not this time. You're still on probation. You're looking at real time here—years."

Peters ashed his cigarette and said nothing.

"Who's your supplier?" Ladd asked again.

"I'm telling you, man, I don't know."

Ladd closed the file and stood up.

"Fine—enjoy prison."

"I want the charges dropped," Peters said.

You're not as dumb as you look, Ladd thought. He sat down again.

"Give me something I don't already know. If you waste my time I'm leaving."

Peters smoked.

"Let's start with a name," Ladd said.

Peters butted his cigarette in the ashtray.

"Can I have another smoke?"

"A name," Ladd said.

Peters sighed.

"Eddie."

"Eddie Smythe?" Ladd said, rolling his eyes so that Peters saw it. "AKA Jimmy S.? You'll need to do better than that."

"Give me another smoke."

Ladd dug into the pack, lit the cigarette and passed it to him.

"Montreal," Peters said.

"What about it?"

"That's where he gets it."

"A name," Ladd said.

"I don't want nobody knowing this came from me."

"A name," Ladd insisted.

"I could get clipped for this," Peters said.

He was breaking and Ladd knew it.

"Listen to you," Ladd said, chuckling to himself. "All gangsta and shit. Aren't you from the Valley? Where'd you go to high school—K.V.?"

Peters huffed.

Ladd huffed back.

"Frickin valley boy."

Peters smoked.

"I only know his first name."

"Spit it out," Ladd said.

"Victor," Peters said. "That's all I know. He's a ghost."

"What else do you know about him?"

"He's Russian."

"Ukrainian," Ladd said. "But close. We've done our homework, Lee. I know when you're lying to me. Don't lie to me."

"I thought he was Russian," Peters said.

Ladd looked over Peters' file again.

"So your coke comes from Victor—is that what you're telling me?"

"Shit man, everything comes from Victor. You guys don't know that?"

Ladd was still looking over the file.

"And the Saint John connection is Eddie Smythe?"

Peters nodded.

"How does he get it?" Ladd asked.

Peters adjusted himself in the chair.

"He flies to Montreal and takes the Greyhound back to Saint John. Once a month—three or four suitcases at a time."

Ladd looked up.

"He goes directly to Victor?"

Peters nodded and smoked.

"They pick him up at the airport and drive him straight to the bus station."

✧

Ladd was sitting in his unmarked cruiser outside Eddie's apartment. He'd been there since dawn. A digital camera with a telescopic lens sat on the dash. He'd taken several pictures already; the building, a bird on a mailbox, and even a chip bag. He was thinking of Lee Peters. And the name Victor. Victor Kravec, Ukrainian mafia boss out of Montreal. Kravec had his hand in just about all of the narcotics trade in Quebec and Atlantic Canada. The biker gangs even had to go through him. And so Ladd was not surprised to hear his name. The problem was making the connection from Eddie Smythe to Victor. Victor was elusive; like Peters had said, a ghost. But if what Peters said was true—that Eddie got his supply directly from Victor—they could trail him to Montreal and make the connection. They got a warrant and tapped Eddie's phone. Then, just three days in, Victor called and they'd deciphered his calling to say good-bye just as Eddie had. Eddie needed to be brought in. But he had up and vanished, and Ladd now sat in his car outside Eddie's apartment, waiting for him to return.

    Detective Harry Ross knocked on the passenger window and opened the door. Ross had an old man dinginess to him; he smelled like coffee stains and his teeth were yellow. He was heavy-set and the car sank a little when he plunked into the seat. He'd retired four years ago. His last job had been Ladd's first. Ross had mentored him, and now he would occasionally find Ladd and tag along. Yesterday he'd spoken to Ladd about Eddie, and Ladd had half expected Ross to show up this morning.

    "Any sign of him?"

    "Not yet," Ladd said.

    "He could be in Montreal," Ross said.

    "That's the last place he'd go."

    Ross folded his newspaper and tossed it into the backseat. "You had breakfast yet? How long you been here? Won't do you much good sitting here all morning."

    Ladd sighed, thinking of a way to agree without agreeing, when in his rear view mirror a Chrysler 300 appeared. It passed slowly and stopped a half block away. Quebec plates. They watched as Ivan and

Dmitri got out and went inside. Ladd snatched the camera and snapped a few pictures. Five minutes later, Charlie dashed from the building and down the street.

Ross frowned.

"Who the hell's that?"

Ladd shrugged.

"He went in this morning—I thought he lived there."

Ivan and Dmitri stepped out and climbed into their car.

Ladd and Ross kept their distance as they trailed the Chrysler uptown and parked along the water. They followed them into Reggie's. Ivan and Dmitri didn't pay them any attention when they sat two tables away. Ladd's back was to them but he could hear their voices. Ross could see them over Ladd's shoulder.

"The tall one just stuck a tack on the wall."

"Ukraine?" Ladd said.

Ross nodded.

"It's them," Ladd said.

"No shit."

They got up and skipped across the street, to the entrance at City Hall where they could still see the diner.

"You stay here," Ladd said. He pointed across King Street, to the TD Bank. "I'll be over there." He made his way over to the bank and stood near the window, next to an ATM. He was pleased with himself for setting this up, for Ross doing as he asked without complaint. He was also pleased to be actually doing something; he'd sat in his car for too long on too many stakeouts where nothing ever happened—sometimes waiting all night, or all day, watching a building, a doorway, a window. But this, this was something; this was fun.

Chapter 9

Walter's back started to ache, sitting in the chair at Wiggins Funeral Home. His head hurt. His chest hurt. Everything hurts, he thought. He desperately wanted to go home, but he couldn't just yet. He couldn't come and then leave right away. It wasn't right. Eddie didn't deserve that. And so he sat, anxious, between the two big windows.

By the time Eddie was fifteen he came and went as he pleased, and Walter had had enough.

"I got another call from your school today. They said you haven't been there all week. Are you even going to school anymore?"

Eddie shrugged, put on his jacket and left.

Walter fell into the couch. He didn't know what to do—nor did he care anymore. A month later, he found a baggie in Eddie's jeans. He hadn't actually seen marijuana before but he knew what it was.

"It's not mine," Eddie had said.

"I'm not a fool, Eddie!"

"Oh no?" Eddie said. "I know what you do with that portrait of Mom—I can hear you at night talking to her! I've known for years!"

Walter could feel his face getting red.

"Don't change the subject," he said.

Eddie shrugged.

"Sure, sure," Walter said. "Shrug it off like you do with everything else in your life. If you were my own child I'd—"

"I'm not your own child."

"No shit," Walter said. "NO SHIT! YOU THINK I SIGNED UP FOR THIS? MY GOD, THE WORST THING ABOUT LOSING MY SISTER WAS INHERITING YOU!"

Eddie looked down at the floor, nodding half to himself, half to Walter.

Walter sighed, his words still hovering over them.

"I didn't mean that," he said. He sighed again and went into the kitchen. He heard the front door open then close, and Eddie was gone. A week passed. Then another. Before he knew it, he hadn't seen or heard from Eddie in a month. And soon a year passed. And another. And Walter had settled back into the routine he'd had before Iris's death. Every now and then he would think of Eddie, but it would pass. He didn't even know if he still lived in the city.

Walter leaned forward in the chair, Eddie's body in front of him, the bridge behind him, and somewhere in the middle there he was, not part of either anymore. It saddened him how easily he'd abandoned his nephew, how he'd let his sister down. It's the guilt that hurts, he thought. And that's never going away. You had your chance with him and you blew it. He turned and looked out the window, unable to face the casket. The bridge looked further away than it actually was; suddenly a distant, unfamiliar thing.

Walter had slid open the toll booth's window as far as it would go, letting in the cold hard wind of the dock, the exhaust fumes, and the smells of the oiled pier and the seaweed on the rocks under the bridge. And he breathed it in. When he got home that evening he collected his morning newspaper by the front door; he hadn't read it yet, a routine he'd broken and hadn't realized it until then.

One day to go and I'm already falling apart.

Relax, Iris said. We're home now. We have what's left of the evening and all the night ahead. What shall we have for dinner? Something nice, to lighten the mood.

Macaroni casserole with garlic bread, Walter said.

Do you have wine? We should get some wine.

Walter's chest rumbled with excitement. He took the bus downtown, to the liquor store at Prince Edward Square. There were small signs on the shelves. AUSTRALIA, FRANCE, CALIFORNIA, ARGENTINA. He grabbed a bottle of Shiraz. I don't know how to pick a good bottle, or what a good bottle is. Do I go by price or do I pick the fanciest label? What was the name of that wine you always drank—the one with the blue bottle? I can never think of it.

It was easy to talk to Iris when he slipped her under his coat, without moving his lips, without making a sound. He put the Shiraz back on the shelf and thought of the tolls again.

You'll be fine, Iris said.

Then another voice came into his head; the voice that always came when he least wanted it to. It said the same thing every time: she's dead.

Go away, Walter said. He felt the portrait in his jacket, the coolness of the metal-plated backing against his chest.

Pick a bottle from France, Iris said.

She's dead, the voice said again.

Shut up!

Maybe a Bordeaux, Iris said.

You're mad.

Walter made his way over to the French wines. Give me this, for now, please.

That one with the black label, Iris said. How much is it?

Don't answer, the voice said.

Or the one with the red label, Iris said. It's a merlot. I hear merlot is dry but we'll only have a glass or two.

Listen to yourself—she can't drink it!

Walter eyed a bottle that said CHATEAU MARGAUX and thought it sounded fancy. How about this one?

Don't do it, the voice said.

It's only twelve bucks, Walter shrugged.

You fool.

I don't care, Walter said. It feels good. It makes me happy.

She's not real.

Why does that matter?

Because for years you've lived in that other place, the voice said. And you know that isn't good—no matter how good it feels. You remember that man in King Square last summer; at first you thought he was talking on a cell phone but then you knew he was talking to himself, and then arguing, and then screaming and everyone was watching as he pranced around, in and out of the fountain screaming at the pigeons. And you remember how people were laughing at him.

If I start arguing with myself I think I'll know, Walter said.

Consider yourself informed, the voice said.

But I'm talking to you.

I am you, the voice said.

But so is she.

She's not. She's madness—a reflection.

Walter huffed. How in Christ do you not go crazy in this city in the winter? There's no colour in anything—it's all grey—the sky and the street, the cold and the muck and slush and shit—how do you not pretend to be somewhere else?

It's more than seasonal and you know it, the voice said. Buy your wine and go home and get drunk like everyone else.

CHATEAU MARGAUX it is! Iris said.

For a split second Walter didn't know that it was Iris who'd spoken and it unnerved him a little that both voices had become one. He headed to the cash.

"Is this a good bottle of wine?" he asked. It felt strange talking to a real person now, using his real voice, the loudness of it, the intimacy gone.

The clerk was an older man, his hair greasy and parted to the side. He squinted and read the label.

"Looks pretty good to me."

Walter paid and went out into the street.

You've got to stop this, the voice said.

Leave me alone, Walter said, relieved that he could again discern the two voices.

Yes, goodbye to him, Iris said.

He caught the bus back to the West Side. When the bus slowed at the tolls Walter turned away so the operator didn't see him. When he got home he perched Iris on the coffee table and lit a Colt cigar and opened the newspaper—the one he'd forgotten to read in the morning. It felt strange to be reading it now. The first thing he saw was the headline **HARBOUR BRIDGE DEAL SEALED.** He sunk a little lower into the couch and sighed.

The alarm clock buzzed at 5:30 the next morning. Walter rolled over and rubbed the sleep from his eyes. Iris was on the pillow next to him.

Do you remember when we were kids and we used to shut off the lights and play with the flashlight under the covers?

You said it felt like being underwater, Iris said.

I'd get a toque and pretend I was Jacques Cousteau.

We were very young, Iris said.

It goes by so fast, Walter said. You blink and all you've got left are memories.

And regret.

That too, Walter said. He stared up at the ceiling. His head spun a little.

Are you nervous? Iris asked.

It's just another day.

But you said the newspaper was going to be there and the TV news and that you were told to look sharp.

That was mostly for Jack—they don't want him showing up too hungover—or drunk—I wouldn't put it past him today.

And now it's you who's hungover.

I'm fine—just a bit of a headache.

Drink some water, Iris said.

Walter waited for his head to clear before he got out of bed. He was anxious, not at working his last shift; he'd worried enough about that already, but his boss had wanted him to be in the booth when the last paying car crossed the tolls. And with newspapermen snapping pictures and TV cameras all around he hoped he'd be okay.

You'll be fine, Iris said.

He went downstairs to the entranceway for the morning paper and tossed it on the coffee table before going into the kitchen for a glass of water. He would skip breakfast this morning; the thought of eggs made his stomach turn.

On his way to the bedroom he saw that he'd overthrown the paper and it had scattered on the floor. As he bent to pick it up his eye caught the name **SMYTHE** in one of the sections. He opened it and there it was: **SMYTHE, EDWARD JAMES JR.** It did not fully sink in, what he was reading, not until he'd finished it and read it through again. For a few seconds the room went still. Then he blinked and everything was normal again. He went into the spare bedroom, to the closet, and under a pile of neatly folded blankets was a box of Eddie's belongings. He brought it into the living room, its weight reminding him of what was in there; these things he'd kept; things he could access whenever he wanted but hadn't till now; half-forgotten things now instantly precious. He placed the box on the coffee table and opened it. LEGO and GI Joe and dinky cars. He knew that these things—just as Iris's belongings had felt when he'd first gone to her house—now belonged to a time he was no longer part of, and a feeling of loneliness dropped like a weight into his chest.

I'm here, Iris said.

Walter stared blankly into the box.

Eddie was a grown man, Iris said.

You're saying that to make me feel better, Walter said. I'm saying that to make me feel better.

He listened for the other voice, hoping for it, but it wasn't there. Then he went into the bathroom and rinsed his face under the sink. Outside was the Reversing Falls and the black of the gorge and the smoke of the pulp mill. He looked down the stretch of the harbour, to the toll bridge, where a few cars crossed, their lights flickering faintly through the rails.

As he got dressed he suddenly realized he'd done this every morning for over thirty-five years and now, right now, would be the last time. This day can't get any worse, he thought. Then he turned and stubbed his toe on the edge of the bed.

Clear everything from your mind, Iris said. Think of how wonderful last night was, how good it felt to have your head tingly and not to be thinking about work—you won't have that to think about anymore. Tonight we can do it all over again.

He stepped into the hallway and down the stairs and outside. It was a cold morning, but not bitter, and he knew, he could feel it, the stillness in the air, that it was going to snow today.

It will be pretty with the snow falling over the bridge, Iris said.

Let me just walk, Walter said.

You can't ignore me.

Please, just give me this one last morning. You tell me to think of something else and now that I'm doing it you start talking to me.

I'm sorry.

Stop talking!

He took his place in the booth and pulled Iris out and perched her up on the counter. Flurries started in the morning. By mid-afternoon the snow fell thick and white and slantwise in the wind. Cars came and went, and inside the booth it was warm and comfortable and Iris kept him company, just as she did every other day.

I told you the snow would look pretty over the bridge, she said. It's so pretty when it falls thick—everything looks so clean and new.

It just covers it up, Walter said.

I don't care, Iris said. I like how the whiteness makes the water look so black, and the pier too.

Walter liked it too; liking it was better than thinking of the dirtiness underneath; of all the dirtiness in his life. The thought of his nephew felt like a weight in his chest.

At quarter to four, Jack Jones entered the booth, the bulk of his huge frame, his huge personality, fitting snug. He pulled out a pint of whiskey.

"I just seen a newspaper guy in the office—Earl was gettin interviewed and you should'a seen him—stiff as a goddam corpse."

Walter thought of Eddie and his heart sank.

"Is that all?" he asked, trying not to show his disappointment. "Just one reporter?"

"There was a cameraman too," Jack said. "But this ain't Festival by the Sea. What were you expectin—a friggin parade?" He poured a dash of whiskey into Walter's mug then took a swig from the pint. Walter eyed the whiskey then drank it down. It burned his throat.

"I thought there might be a few people wanting to see the last car come through."

"Ha!" Jack laughed. "You think they're gonna put out a big red ribbon for the last car or somethin? I'll do it—put me in the goddam paper!"

The cameraman came out and stood beside the booth, capturing the cars as they passed. The reporter stood opposite the booth and snapped a few pictures. And then they were gone.

Their boss, Earl, knocked on the booth and poked his head inside.

"That's it—shut 'er down."

Then he was gone too.

"Now what?" Walter said.

"Go home and relax," Jack said. "Enjoy your days. Hire one of those topless cleaning ladies and get her to polish your pecker." He poured another dash of whiskey into Walter's mug then raised the pint and drank. On his way out he patted Walter on the shoulder. "Nice workin with you, Walt—come on by to the Three Mile sometime and say hello. I got a job workin the door."

Walter raised the barrier so the cars could pass without stopping. A car came and the driver tossed his token into the basket.

"It's done," Walter said, but the driver never heard him.

I know it hurts, Iris said.

Walter huffed.

That's not what hurts right now. My nephew—your son—is lying dead over at Wiggins. He squinted and could see, across the harbour and faintly through the snow, the outline of Wiggins Funeral Home. He stepped out of the booth and into the cold. The snow fell into his eyes. Enough of this, he thought. Go home. Eat. Go see Eddie. Poor Eddie. The poor boy. It hurts too much to think of.

And with that, Walter left the tolls for the last time. The sidewalk was smoothed over white with snow. A few hundred meters down the road he turned and looked back but he could not see the tolls, just the faint glow of the bridge and a car whose lights emerged from the whiteness and passed him by.

Chapter 10

Charlie's heart was still racing after he got back from Eddie's apartment. It hadn't sunk in at first; what he'd just done, but once he got upstairs and cracked a can of beer and was sitting on his couch in the safety of his apartment, he knew how real and how dangerous the whole thing was.

He slumped on his couch, an old couch with the soft flat cushions, and drank, the beer cold and fresh in his mouth. His apartment looked and smelled like a used bookstore. Paperbacks were stacked on the floor, the coffee table, and along the windowsill. Two bookshelves stood on the wall beside the window, with everything from Hemingway to Hustler. He scanned the spines for *Crime and Punishment*, spotted it, plucked it and looked for the passage he'd thought of in Eddie's bathroom. He felt like Raskolnikov again; it was as drab outside as Dostoyevsky's St. Petersburg and he wondered how he was going to face it. It's not that bad, he told himself. It's Friday, you've taken a shit, had a beer and almost gotten killed and it's not even nine o'clock. This afternoon you'll go out with Prin and she'll tell you about your daughter—Jesus, your daughter—your living, breathing, crying, smiling, laughing real-life daughter. Forget about outside. Summer is right around the corner. You always do this to yourself—you let it bring you down. Not today. He opened another beer and laid down on the couch and started *Crime and Punishment* from the beginning. He hadn't read it in years. He drank and read and then drank some more, and then dozed.

Prin had taken Daisy to April's and then had cleaned her apartment, tucking Daisy's toys in her toy box, sweeping the floors and finishing the last of the dishes from breakfast. She was feeling better, physically at least, which helped her forget about things for short periods of time. And she was excited about seeing Charlie. Excited and nervous. She'd lied to him and she realized she'd have to tell him the truth about who she was, what she still was. Now that he knew about Daisy, he was going to be in her life forever. Or was he? Did he even care? When she thought of this a small piece of her regretted telling him; that the tiny bubble she and Daisy had been living in, had burst. But she had to tell him; he had a daughter and she knew, eventually, that Charlie had to be told, that this day was going to come sooner or later. It was the right thing to do. She wondered if he'd hate her for not telling him. Would he try to take Daisy away from her? Would he want custody? She didn't even know what kind of person Charlie was anymore. Had she ever known him? No, she thought. You knew him for one weekend. Anyone can fake it for a weekend. And just look at how much you've changed since then. But you've changed for the better, she thought. And maybe he has too. And maybe he wasn't faking it. Maybe he was a good person after all. She kept telling herself this as she made a cup of tea and turned on the TV, trying to clear her head of all the things of the past two days.

By the time Charlie left to get Prin in the afternoon it was snowing hard; the roads were slick and his car skidded in and out of the tracks. Prin was waiting at her door, nestled under the alcove. Charlie thought that she looked very pretty with the snow falling around her. She was dressed in a red wool coat with big red buttons, and she'd kept her hands in her pockets as she skipped over the sidewalk, careful not to slip. She had a white toque with a pompom and the ends of hair fell around her ears and on the back of her neck.

Charlie noticed the freckles on her nose—the whiteness of the toque brought them out, and her eyes—he didn't remember them being so big and so bright. But she's older now, he thought. She's not a teenager anymore—but a woman—a mother. When he remembered this he felt her eyes, though beautiful, now looked tired, almost sad, and the youthful vibrancy he thought he'd seen a moment ago was gone.

Prin smiled and buckled her seatbelt.

"Where are you taking me?"

"You'll see."

The car skidded through the snowy uptown streets. They parked at the top of Princess Street. The sidewalk was slippery as they walked along, the snow flicking in their eyes. Prin looked down to the harbour, to the outline of the bridge.

"It's hard to believe today's the last day of the tolls. It's sad in a way, don't you think?"

Charlie slipped a bit in the snow.

"People want it."

"I know," Prin said. "But it's still sad to see the end of it. I notice these kinds of things more since I've had Daisy. She went through so many stages growing up—first it was crawling, then walking, then talking. It was hard when each stage ended because I knew I'd never see it again." She stopped and turned, facing Charlie. "Do you hate me for not telling you, Charles? Because if you do, I understand."

"I don't hate you."

"But the first part—when she was a baby—you'll never know any of that."

"I don't like dirty diapers," Charlie said.

They rounded the corner at Prince William Street where Charlie led her into the Bourbon Quarter. Prin's eyes brightened when they stepped inside.

"I've never been here before."

The cozy restaurant had the look and feel of a New Orleans eatery; the aromas of Cajun cuisine from the open kitchen at the back; the old style charm in the worn oak beams, the brick wall and brasswork of the bar that ran the length of the room opposite a row of booths, now empty; only the cook in the kitchen, a waitress behind the bar putting away a tray of glasses, and Shawn, who stepped out from behind the bar.

"How you doing, Charlie—and this must be Prin."

Prin grinned. Her cheeks were red from the cold.

They sat in a booth with a bouquet of daisies on the table.

Prin smiled, a girlish smile, her shoulders raised.

"Are these for me?"

"Maybe," Charlie said.

Prin looked around.

"It's so cozy in here."

"They normally don't serve the dinner menu till later," Charlie said. "But Shawn's an old friend."

Prin's eyes started to water. She blinked to clear them without Charlie seeing. She'd stopped hurting down there, and it had stopped bleeding, but she regretted not telling Charlie the truth about her. When Charlie had said that it was good that she was done with all of that, she'd said nothing. You lied by not saying anything, she thought. And here you are, lying to him still. What would he think of you if he knew you were still doing it? Would he try to get custody of Daisy? It terrified her to think of going to court and having to show how she supported herself. She'd lose her. Just the thought of that was painful enough. But Charlie made her smile a little in the warmth of the restaurant, with the snow falling outside in big thick flakes and how good it felt to be just sitting, about to have a meal and a drink in the afternoon. Don't tell him, she thought. Not yet—not with him trying so hard to please you. Try to forget it for now, for just this afternoon—just until the snow stops.

Charlie ordered a bottle of wine.

Prin smiled again.

"Is life good, Charles?"

"It could be worse."

The waitress came with the wine and filled their glasses.

Charlie held up his glass.

"A toast—to new beginnings."

Prin liked the sound of that.

"To new beginnings," she said, and their glasses clinked. She took a sip of wine and looked out to the falling snow.

"You seem nervous," Charlie said.

"I am."

"Why?"

"I've never been on a date before."

"Come on."

"Not a real date—not one where I don't have to pretend."

Tell him, she thought. It will be good for you to tell him.

"So why did you quit?" Charlie asked.

She lifted her glass and took a drink, not a sip this time.

"Let's talk of something else. I'm having too nice of a time to talk about ugly things." She looked down at the menu. "I have no idea what I want."

Charlie looked over the menu.

"Alright, let's see...How about we start with the crab cakes. Then the rack of lamb—no, the duck."

Prin found it on the menu.

"I've never had duck before. Lacquered duck breast with a sweet and sour glaze. Sounds yummy."

"You'll love it," Charlie said.

Prin's eyes started to water again.

"What's wrong?" Charlie asked.

"Nothing, Charles. Everything is perfect." She wiped her eyes with a tissue, dabbing at her Mascara. "I must look silly crying—do you see?—I really am nervous—I don't even know how to act. Just look at me."

"Just be you," Charlie said.

Prin started crying.

"I'm so sorry."

"Oh shut up," Charlie said.

"I'm not the same person, Charles. I'm not that foolish girl you once knew. I grew up."

"Yes, you did," Charlie said.

"I'm a good mother, Charles."

"I'm sure you are."

Prin shifted her napkin, placing it perfectly in front of her.

"I really am. Daisy is such a happy little girl. She knows I love her more than anything and that I'll always be there for her—that I'd never leave her or mess it up. A mother is supposed to keep her child from harm—or from seeing harm—even in herself. Daisy can feel it—even as a little girl she can see more than what you think. It's tricky, but I've learned to mask it."

"Mask what?" Charlie said.

Prin dabbed her eyes with the tissue.

"My own sadness, I suppose."

"Daisy's a lucky little girl to have you," Charlie said.

"Do you think so?"

"I do."

"For real?"

"For real."

Prin tucked the tissue into her purse.

"Thank you, Charles. I need to hear that sometimes. I go crazy worrying about it." She smiled sadly. "Things have happened to me."

"Things have happened to all of us," Charlie said.

"But I mean bad things—not just life."

She was about to cry again but the waitress came. The snow was falling heavily out the window and there was piano music playing and she felt the wine inside her and she tingled and tucked the lie away; it wasn't the right time for something like that; it would ruin everything. She felt safe here, in the coziness of it all, with Charlie.

"I thought you didn't want to talk about ugly things," Charlie said. "So tell me something good. What are you doing now?"

Prin sipped her wine.

"I'm a tour guide."

Charlie grinned.

"Good for you. Do you do the cruise ships when they come in the summer?"

Prin nodded and sipped again.

"Are you still delivering milk?"

Charlie shook his head.

"I'm a mailman now. All I needed was a strong back and a weak mind." He grinned again. "It's not so bad. I've got an allowance for gas. It's nice having my own car."

"Look at us," Prin said. "All grown up."

"Never!" Charlie said, grinning still.

The crab cakes came and smelled of dill and the salty smell of the air in the summer. Prin's mouth watered. Charlie filled her wine glass and scooped one onto her plate. The snow kept falling. Charlie worried about the roads and he told himself not to drink too much. He felt better when he told himself this, but the snow kept falling and he kept drinking. They ate and drank and laughed and the duck came and Prin loved it, just as Charlie had said, and it was all such a perfect afternoon.

Chapter 11

After Ivan and Dmitri had finished their breakfasts they stepped out onto Germain Street. The bridge was a misty grey outline in the harbour. Ivan lit a cigarette. He was feeling better from the coffee, re-energized, his eyes no longer itchy from being awake all night. His body ached but with the caffeine and all the day ahead he was in a good mood as he walked. He could see up close the old brick buildings he'd seen from his car earlier in the morning. There was the smell of the harbour and a cold wind swirling through the streets. He pulled out his book and skimmed through it. Dmitri had his hands in his pockets, his chin tucked under his collar.

"Where to first?" Ivan said, the cigarette moving with his lips.

Dmitri shrugged.

Ivan flipped to the center of the book, to the map of downtown. He pointed up the hill.

"The City Market should be up that way."

They hiked all the way up the steep ascent of King Street, level with King Square and its tall oak trees black and bare, and at the centre of the square, the bandstand, tall and magnificent, its roof green with age. They walked right past the same bench Prin had met April and Daisy feeding pigeons, to the two-storey bandstand with its rows of cobblestones circling the empty fountain. Ivan read the plaque. "A MEMORIAL TO EDWARD VII KING-EMPEROR 1901-1910. GIFT OF CITY CORNET BAND TO THE CITY OF SAINT JOHN, NOVEMBER 2ND, 1909."

Dmitri shivered.

"King Kong," he said.

A few sparse flakes fell here and there as they crossed the street and into the warmth and humidity of the market and its morning aromas; seafood chowder simmering in big pots, fish lined silver in ice, the black bunches of clams and mussels, bacon and eggs, ground coffee and buttery breads and rolls. There was a steady murmur, the flow of locals, shopping, chatting, passing through, the smoothness of the slanted cement floor, the shops with trinkets and books and collectables, and high above, the whiteness of the timbers and beams, and the white light of the windows bright through the beams.

Ivan looked up, half reading from his book, half talking to Dmitri.

"Says the roof is supposed to be an inverted keel to incorporate the shipbuilding that was big here back then—one of the leading shipbuilding centres in the world." He looked up at the beams, at the whiteness of the outside light coming in.

"I'm getting a coffee," Dmitri said. "You want one?"

Ivan nodded.

Dmitri found him a few minutes later in the centre aisle, still looking up at the beams. By the time they walked the length of the market and stepped outside it was snowing a little more. Ivan lit another cigarette. He was reading again from his book as they crossed King Street and stepped onto Prince William, taking his time walking a few blocks in.

"This is one of the most beautiful Victorian streetscapes in Canada."

"It's a bunch of buildings," Dmitri said.

"Beautiful buildings," Ivan said.

"Old buildings."

"Historical buildings."

Dmitri spit onto the street.

"What the hell's got into you? Can't we just walk around without the guided tour? I don't give a shit about this place—all the history and all that shit—it doesn't interest me. I'm sorry—it just doesn't. And I don't know why it interests you all of a sudden."

Ivan sighed.

"I'm tired and you're making it worse."

Dmitri spit again.

"Alright. Sure."

"There's a building around here with gargoyles," Ivan said.

"Gargoyles are cool."

Ivan smoked and shook his head.

"Jesus, you're just like a little kid."

Twenty minutes after Ladd and Ross had left Reggie's and had placed themselves in view of the restaurant—Ladd inside the TD Bank across King Street, Ross at the City Hall—Ivan and Dmitri started down Germain Street. Ross stepped out and followed them up King Street. He looked over at Ladd who motioned for him to keep going. Ross skipped ahead to catch up while Ladd walked up the opposite side of the street. They followed them into King Square, where Ivan and Dmitri had stopped in front of the bandstand, then into the market, the whoosh of the warm air sweeping over them. Ivan was looking up at the rafters.

Ross huffed.

"They're a couple of tourists."

"They're up to something," Ladd said.

Ross looked up to the ceiling.

"What's he looking at?"

"I have no idea."

"Suppose they're terrorists?"

Ladd rolled his eyes.

"They're not terrorists."

"They are to Eddie Smythe," Ross said. "If they find him before we do."

Chapter 12

In the afternoon the parking lot at Wiggins Funeral Home was plowed and salted, the snow pushed to the perimeters, but it had kept snowing and there was now a fine layer that smoothed white over the lot, with dark patches throughout, where the salt was thickest. Jeremy stood in the front foyer and looked at his watch. Eddie was late for everything but with the snow falling and the streets as slippery as they were, it was understandable. Jeremy smiled to himself, realizing Eddie was late for his own funeral. When Eddie finally arrived he handed him a coffee and a box of Timbits.

"Thanks for doing all this, man."

Eddie brushed the snow off his jacket and kicked his boots together and looked around the foyer. His mouth opened slightly, and he stood, silent.

"You okay?" Jeremy asked.

"I remember this place," Eddie said. "My parents were here. It's weird. I remember it different—it felt bigger."

Jeremy took him gently by the arm.

"We don't have a lot of time."

Eddie shook his head, snapping out of his trance. He grinned.

"Look at you, man—all business eh?"

Jeremy *was* all business now. If this was going to work he needed everything to look and feel like a real wake. He was dressed in a suit and tie and he talked the way he did when at work; there was no *man* or *dude* or *bro* to be found in his vocabulary here.

He led Eddie through the foyer, to the back of the building and into the basement, to a room with a long table and eight green conference chairs, and beyond them an assortment of opened caskets, lit by pot lights, the whiteness of the cushions and the polished wood shining in the light. The room had the aura of a VIP room, but without the music and without the girls; the way such a room might look and feel after the music has stopped and the night has ended.

"Take your pick," Jeremy said. "Don't choose something too expensive because they won't believe it."

Eddie laughed as he perused the caskets.

"This is like buying a car."

"Exactly," Jeremy said. "Pick the one you can afford."

Eddie ran his fingers along the edge of a dark oak casket with a silk lining.

"This one."

Jeremy shook his head.

"Try the one in the corner," he said, nodding to a thin, cedar casket.

Eddie huffed.

"That looks cheap as hell."

"That's why it's perfect," Jeremy said. "Now help me get it down."

They lifted it off the shelf and placed it on the floor.

"Take your shoes off," Jeremy said.

Eddie slipped out of his shoes and into the casket, rested his head on the pillow and closed his eyes. Then he held out his arms and very slowly, sat up. "Nosferatu, man!" He had a big grin. "I could sleep in this thing."

"Don't worry," Jeremy said. "You will."

Then Eddie frowned.

"Won't they see me breathing?"

"It's all about perception," Jeremy said. "And all that takes is suggestion; you just need to *look* dead. If someone sees you breathing they won't think they saw it; they'll only need to think you're dead for you to be dead in their heads, and if you're dead in their heads you're dead for real—to them anyway—and that's all that matters."

Carol Wiggins entered the room. She was dressed in black stretch pants and a black top, and her hair was black and she had thick black eyeliner. Her lip was pierced and with the paleness of her face and the black of her lipstick the metal ring was very noticeable.

"Dad left instructions for the Bertrand wake for tomorrow. They left a number in case we need anything." She looked down at Eddie in the casket. "What's this about again?"

"Never mind," Jeremy said. "It's just a prank we're playing on some friends."

"Dad would kill you if he ever found out."

"But he won't—right?"

"Relax," Carol said. "When do you need me to do it?"

"The wake starts at six."

Carol eyed Eddie.

"It might take me a bit longer than normal—I've got to find the right colours—I've never had to make someone look dead before."

"We've got a few things to do upstairs," Jeremy said. "I'll bring him down as soon as we're done." He looked down at Eddie. "Come on—we've got work to do." They carried the casket to the elevator, then into the viewing room and placed it in the corner. Jeremy went into the hall and returned with a vacuum cleaner. "Here—do the whole room."

Eddie looked down at the carpet.

"You joking, man? It's so clean I can see the footprints."

"Exactly—get rid of them. There should only be vacuum marks."

Eddie plugged the vacuum into the wall and started. Jeremy left and returned with two flower bouquets and placed them on the floor along the wall. He left then returned with more.

"Do the *whole* floor—not just the footprints—you can only see vacuum lines in a few places and so it looks like you didn't do the whole thing. Start at one end and make your way across the room."

"Come on, man—this is a big room."

Jeremy left and returned with a can of Lysol and a rag and raised his voice over the hum of the vacuum: "AROUND THE WINDOW-SILLS AND THE END TABLES." He set up the bouquets about the room; on the stands at each end of the casket, the end tables along the far wall between the windows. He filled a dish with mints, filled a jug of water, and replaced a tissue box with a new one. In the front foyer was a pegboard sign and he changed it to:

SMYTHE, EDWARD JAMES JR
6PM TO 9PM
ROOM 2

When he returned to the viewing room Eddie was wiping down the windowsills. The carpet looked good. Jeremy lit a scented candle and placed it on the floor in the doorway. This was something his father had taught him—to never put it in the room, but place it on the floor in between both rooms and light it for no more than fifteen minutes. This way the scent would to be present, but not strong—just a hint—nothing more than a hint. He inspected the room one last time and was satisfied.

"Put the vacuum away and follow me." He led Eddie out the front doors, handed him a shovel that was perched near the entrance, next to a bag of salt. "Clear off the steps and spread the salt. And be generous with it."

Eddie gave him an exaggerated military salute then went to work.

A short while later Eddie came inside and Jeremy led him into the basement. Carol was listening to her iPod. Jeremy tapped her on the shoulder and she jumped in surprise then plucked the headphones from her ears.

"Lay down on the floor," she said to Eddie. She knelt beside him and opened her make-up kit and picked through a variety of foundations. "You'll need to look pale, almost white—I'll put a layer of powder to start with, then a layer of rose to look like we're trying to give you some colour.

Your skin is pale to begin with so it shouldn't be too hard. I'll give you a good thick coat all over so it's important not to move your face once I put it on, otherwise it'll crack and I'll have to do it over again." She sat up and squinted, examining Eddie's face. "I'm not sure about the lips. They'll have to be purple, almost blue—I think maybe some wax to coat them, then some blue and red, but not till after you're asleep—you can't move your lips once it's on."

"Just do whatever you've got to do to make him look dead," Jeremy said.

Carol glanced up at her brother.

"I had nothing to do with this if you get busted."

"Relax," Jeremy said.

Carol set out an assortment of foundations, eyeliners, lipsticks, wax, and blush, all in rows beside her on the floor. She stretched up to the counter and grabbed her iPod and looked up at Jeremy again.

"Leave me alone and let me do my work." She swiped at him as sisters do to their brothers. "NOW."

Chapter 13

The snow had blanketed the city by the time Charlie and Prin left the Bourbon Quarter and made their way back up Princess Street to Charlie's car, now buried in a layer of wet snow. Charlie cleared the windows and the car skidded out onto the street.

"The duck was yummy," Prin said.

Charlie's fingers were red from clearing the snow and he blew on them to warm them up.

"I told you you'd like it."

"What's next?"

"Part two," Charlie said. "It's a surprise."

They drove slowly through the city and out to the highway where they lost themselves in the snow.

"It's really coming down," Charlie said.

"You're not taking me out on the river again, are you?"

"No," Charlie said. He was grinning.

"What?" Prin said.

"It kind of feels like old times."

"It was one time, Charles."

"It was a whole weekend."

Prin grinned a little now too.

"Yes, okay, I'll give you that."

By the time they got off the highway and onto Rothesay Road it was snowing so hard they could not see the river, just a blanket of white out the window. Prin knew the river was out there somewhere, behind the whiteness, and she remembered when Charlie had taken her out on the water just before dawn, and how there'd been a perfect moment between them as the early morning sun made the whole sky red. But now the whiteness made it feel like a world away, a different place from an entirely different time.

Charlie had to squint to see the road. Every now and then he'd recognize a house and know where he was. He turned into the driveway of the old Victorian house with the wraparound veranda. The driveway was smoothened over white with snow, and he was pleased to see the indentations of his tracks only, from yesterday.

"Stay here for a minute," he said and climbed out.

Prin sat in the car and waited. She looked around the yard, at the white of everything, the snow building up on the trees and the power lines and how black the windows of the house looked in all the whiteness.

The front door opened and Charlie waved her over. She climbed out of the car and made her way across the driveway, retracing Charlie's steps in the snow.

"Come on in," Charlie said.

Once inside the house, Prin kicked the snow from off her shoes. She looked around the corridor, at the pictures on the walls and the brightness of the kitchen beyond.

"What is this?"

"Follow me."

"But Charlie, this isn't—"

"Just come here."

Prin followed him into the next room with the big long windows that looked out onto the veranda that had been so black in the snow. Charlie plopped into one of the chairs and motioned for her to sit.

She sat.

"This is it," Charlie said. "Me and you and Daisy in the big house and you a mom and me a dad and Daisy having her friends over for sleepovers and when it's cold outside the fire's burning and we'd cozy up in our chairs and talk about our day and just…be."

Tears were rolling down Prin's cheeks.

Charlie sat up.

"What's wrong? I thought you'd like this."

"I do—it's wonderful."

"Then why are you crying?"

"I'm not the girl you think I am, Charles."

"That's cool," Charlie said. "We've got a lot of catching up to do."

Prin started crying again.

"Two days ago I was raped."

Charlie didn't say a word.

"It was by a client," Prin said.

Charlie frowned.

"I don't understand."

"I lied," Prin said. "I should have told you from the beginning."

Again, Charlie remained silent.

"I don't blame you if you hate me," Prin said.

"I don't hate you."

"Well you should."

"Starting today it's over and done with," Charlie said.

"It's not that easy."

"Sure it is."

"I'm not going to stop, Charles—the money's too good." She wiped her eyes. "I don't go out and look for work—I'm not a hooker anymore. Clients come to me. It's very exclusive."

"Sounds lovely," Charlie said.

His comment annoyed her, and in her annoyance she composed herself.

"It's only a job, Charles. My body still belongs to me."

"Except when you get raped."

"That was the first and only time."

Charlie sighed.

"I don't get it."

Prin crossed her arms defiantly.

"Are you going to pay for Daisy's university? She's not going to drop out of high school like me. She's going to be whatever she wants and I'm going to make sure of that."

"It's not all about money," Charlie said.

"Oh yes it is," Prin said. "I hate to say it, Charles, but money does buy happiness. That's the truth of the world—you sink or you swim. Period."

"Are you happy?"

"It's not about me."

"Are you happy?" Charlie asked again.

"It's not as simple as that," she said. "I like being the one who sacrifices for her. I like being a good mother—that makes me happy. When you become a parent you realize the world isn't about you anymore. You become secondary, even to yourself. You'll have to learn that, Charles."

"And the fact that your own life goes down the shitter," Charlie said. "That makes it okay?"

"When I see that Daisy is happy? Yes. It makes everything tolerable."

"Even what happened to you?"

"Everything," Prin said.

"I don't accept that," Charlie said. "I can't."

Prin shook her head.

"I didn't want this to upset you. These last two days I've been in a bubble. It's the only way I know how to deal with it. But now that I've told you it feels more real than ever."

Charlie breathed.

"I'm real," Charlie said. "And I don't care what you do."

"That's easy to say," Prin said. She started crying again. "Do you remember when you took me out on the river with those two bottles of wine and we saw the sun rise over the trees? Then you jumped into the water and you pulled my arm and I fell in and we splashed each other? And then you grabbed me and we kissed and the water was so cold but we didn't care?"

"Yes," Charlie said. "I haven't forgotten it."

"And the boat started to drift away and we had to swim to catch it?"

"I remember."

"Daisy was in me then and I didn't even know it," Prin said. "She was there that morning with us."

Charlie nodded.

"We'll always have that," Prin said. "We'll always have Daisy." She shuffled her feet and grinned slightly. "I'm a different girl now—but things between us—that hasn't changed. It won't ever change."

Charlie wanted to say No, Prin, you're perfect and you still make my heart flutter the way you did when you were young and foolish and you said these kinds of things all the time, and there was an innocence under everything you said, and I loved you for it then and I love you now still. But he didn't. He simply grinned back at her. It was too soon to say something like that. Or was it? Would there ever be a right time for it? He'd tried, once, that morning she spoke of, out on the river. He'd wanted to tell her there and then that he loved her, but he couldn't; he knew what she'd say, that they were two very different people living very different lives, and he didn't want to hear it, and so he'd kissed her instead, saying it in head as their lips touched, saying it over and over again, until the boat drifted so far away he had to swim to get it, and the chance to tell her seemed to be gone forever. But now here it was again, and he was not letting it slip away this time. He looked her straight in the eye. "Prin—"

"Don't say it, Charles. Please don't say it."

"I love you."

"Oh, Charlie," she said, her eyes filling with tears again. "But how?"

"I just do. And that's all that matters. You do love me, don't you? Or am I being an arse?"

"You're being an arse."

"But you love me?"

"Of course I do."

"Then say it," Charlie said.

Prin was crying again.

"I can't. I'm sorry. You're too nice to me, Charles."

"It's a first date," Charlie said. "I'm just being polite."

Prin smiled.

"You should know that I don't put out on first dates."

"Then I'll stop being nice," Charlie grinned.

Prin became serious again.

"Can it be how it was that summer evening—how it started out on the roof then we went downstairs and made love on the floor, with all the books you showed me—piles of books on the couch and you whispered to me that it felt as if the world was ours—can it be like that?"

"Sure," Charlie said. "Just like that."

Tears streaked down Prin's cheeks.

"Okay then," she said. "I'll put out. But just once—I don't want you getting any ideas."

Charlie laughed and sat back in the chair and looked around the room.

"So this whole thing was a waste of time?"

"No—of course not. But can we get back to just being ourselves? It doesn't work for me—having something like that hanging over everything. I was having such a lovely time today."

"Sure," Charlie said.

"Why does love have to complicate everything?"

Charlie sighed.

"I don't know. I'm sorry I said it."

"Don't be," Prin said. "But let's pretend it didn't happen. Can we do that?"

Charlie checked his watch. It was after five o'clock. It was dark outside. Out the big long windows the snow was letting up. He could see across the lawn to the bare trees in the yard, the cedars at the edge of the

road, and the car's lights pulling into the driveway—
    He grabbed Prin.
    "SHIT!"
    "What's going on?"
    "Get your coat—where is it?"
    "In the kitchen—"
    "I'll grab it—go—quick, through the back door!"
    "Charles, I—"
    "Just get out the back door, quick! I'll get your coat!"
    "But my shoes—"
    "Where are they?"
    "By the front door."
    "SHIT-FUCK! I'll get them! Now go!"
    "I'm sorry—"
    "JUST GO!"
    Prin went out the back door and Charlie scrambled into the kitchen and swept up Prin's coat then into the front foyer for her shoes where he could see Dr. Staal and his wife eyeing his car. He ran back into the kitchen then out the back door onto the veranda where Prin was shivering in the cold, one foot on top of the other. She quickly slipped on her shoes and coat and they crept around the veranda where they peeked their heads out. Dr. Staal and his wife were unloading their luggage, still eyeing Charlie's car.
    Charlie whispered: "Just follow my lead—don't say anything." They wandered out around the house, appearing to Dr. and Mrs. Staal. "Oh there you are! I was here for a delivery and noticed the mail was piling up and went around back to make sure everything was okay."
    "Very well," Dr. Staal said. He was an older man, with hair as white as the snow, and his face was wrinkled and he rarely smiled, which added a sternness to everything he said. "It was kind of you to be looking out for us, but as you can see, we're home now—good day."
    Charlie smiled and he and Prin made their way across the powdery snow to his car. Charlie started it up. The wipers cleared the snow

and they watched as the Staals went inside.

"Do you think they believed us?" Prin asked.

"I doubt it," Charlie said.

"I hope you don't get fired."

"It's a government job," Charlie said. "I can't get fired."

"This has been a fun date."

"I'm glad you're enjoying yourself."

"So what's next?"

"I'll take you home—I've got something to attend to."

"That sounds important," Prin said. She shivered.

"It's nothing really."

"Then tell me."

Charlie told her about Eddie and Jeremy Wiggins, and the wake.

"Can I come?" Prin asked.

"You sure?"

"It sounds like fun."

"It could be dangerous."

"But it would look more real with more people."

"Sure."

"Then I'll go with you," Prin said. She shivered again and held her hands to the vent. "We're fine pretenders, aren't we Charles?"

Eddie had dressed in a shirt and a plaid tie—the only tie he owned—and had taken a Quaalude. And so he was groggy as he climbed into the casket they'd placed in a nook at the far end of the viewing room.

"Tired yet?" Jeremy asked.

"Oh yeah, man. My eyes are pretty heavy right now."

"Don't fight it. This thing starts in twenty minutes and you've got to be out cold."

By the time Charlie and Prin arrived and had found the viewing room, Eddie was asleep, his hands crossed. Carol had applied makeup to his hands, along with a wax coating on his lips which were now the colour of dried berries.

Charlie looked down at the casket.

"Shit, he looks good."

"He's not really dead, right?" Prin said.

Charlie gave Jeremy a quick smile.

"She's with me."

"That's cool," Jeremy said. "I'm thinking you two can wait outside—have a smoke or something. When they come, just act normal."

"I don't smoke," Prin said.

Jeremy leaned over the casket and reached into Eddie's pockets and pulled out a lighter and a pack of cigarettes.

"You do now."

"When do you expect them?" Charlie asked.

"No idea."

"Do you think they'll even come?"

"They'll either come or they're back in Montreal by now," Jeremy said.

Charlie yawned. It had been a long day and this charade wasn't nearly as important to him as what he and Prin had done today—of all they'd talked about—of what Prin had told him, and now, what the two of them had become—or hadn't become, he still wasn't sure. He wandered over to the sofa which sat along the wall by the windows. Prin followed and sat beside him.

"I'm having fun," she said. "Our date isn't over yet, is it? Maybe after this we can get some Coronas and go up on your roof?"

"We'd freeze," Charlie said.

"I don't care—do you have blankets?"

They sat for a few minutes without talking.

Jeremy walked over to them.

"You guys should get out there soon."

Chapter 14

Ladd and Ross had followed Ivan and Dmitri all day. After the City Market they trailed them through the uptown streets, through the hilly Trinity Royal District and its fine collection of nineteenth century urban architecture, stopping for long periods of time as Ivan and Dmitri studied the buildings, Ivan always referring to his book. Then it was down to the waterfront, into the atrium at Market Square, past the fountain where they toured the library and the museum, and finally into Grannan's Restaurant which looked out to the Boardwalk and the lighthouse at the mouth of the harbour, where they ate oysters and jumbo scallops and each picked a lobster from the tank, which Ivan had insisted Dmitri try.

"I'm getting tired of the guided tour," Ross said. "And I'm starving."

"You go on home," Ladd said.

Ross huffed.

"I've been here all day—I'm not leaving now."

They followed them back out to their car and stayed on them, keeping at a distance as they crossed the highway and turned onto Hilyard Street, past the Lord Beaverbrook Rink, its parking lot half-full for a local hockey game. Next they turned onto Chesley Drive, which took them over the Reversing Falls Bridge and into the parking lot at the restaurant on the edge of the gorge. They watched as Ivan and Dmitri went inside.

"They can't be eating again," Ross said.

Ladd frowned.

"Then why else are they here?"

Ivan was reading through his book. Dmitri was not interested. He'd had enough of this city. He let out a sigh as Ivan approached a woman and asked where the platform was. The woman pointed to a door at the back. Ivan led Dmitri out the door and up a set of stairs that led to a platform that overlooked the Reversing Falls Bridge, its steel frame neatly outlined in a puffy layer of snow. It had stopped snowing and high overhead the clouds were passing, opening up the stars and the night sky, and far below, in the gorge, was the water, black and cold.

Ladd and Ross could see them up on the platform. Ladd rolled down his window and snapped a few pictures.

"Maybe they're going to throw him off the bridge."

"Wouldn't be the worst idea ever," Ross said. "Years ago a body washed up near the mill—bloated like a balloon. You couldn't even tell where his eyes and nose were—the skin all black and yellow, covered in seaweed and leeches and gunk, bits of it nibbled away by god-knows-what. They even picked a fish out of his rectum."

"Jesus," Ladd said.

"We figured he'd been down there a couple months," Ross said. "The current pinned him under a ledge or a rock. But that's about all we knew."

"It's not their M.O.," Ladd said, rolling up the window. "It's not a bullet to the head—quick and done."

"Neither is sightseeing," Ross said.

"Maybe they're a decoy."

"I doubt it."

"So what do you think it is?"

Ross shrugged.

"I think these two aren't any closer to finding Eddie Smythe than we are."

Up on the platform, Ivan's eyes were fixed upon the gorge, a cigarette in his mouth, the smoke whirling violently in the wind.

"This is the only place in the world where this happens."

Dmitri looked down.

"Where what happens?"

"The current flows both ways," Ivan said. He flipped through his book. "This is where the St. John River and the Bay of Fundy meet."

Dmitri looked down again, between the slick black rocks, the foam yellow in the dark water, yellow against the white of the snow. He squinted to see it better.

"I don't see anything."

Ivan smiled.

"Me neither. Maybe it's better during the day."

"I doubt it," Dmitri said. He snorted and spit into the blackness.

"But this has been a good day," Ivan said. "All things considered."

Dmitri shrugged.

"Sure."

"We should do these things more often, me and you," Ivan said.

"What are you talking about?" Dmitri frowned.

Ivan smoked his cigarette.

"Nothing," he said. "Never mind."

He tucked the book into his pocket, leaned over the railing and looked down the stretch of the harbour, to the toll bridge and the lights of the city on the other side of the water. He was exhausted, and the cold wind felt fresh and good on his face. He flicked his cigarette into the gorge. Far below, the water swirled and foamed.

Chapter 15

Now that it had stopped snowing, the sky was clear and the moon was very bright. Charlie and Prin hadn't been outside very long before Walter came. He did not look at them when he walked by, up the steps and into the funeral home.

"That must be his uncle," Charlie whispered.

"Does he know?"

"I doubt it," Charlie said. "It's better that he doesn't—for his own good."

Prin kicked at a clump of salt that had melted the snow around it "Do you see, Charles? Sometimes it's better not knowing."

Inside the funeral home, Walter stood over Eddie's body, his winter coat folded over his arm, his hands clasping his toque like a prayer book. He looks like an angel, he thought.

He wasn't an angel, Iris said.

He was when he was with you. I was the one who ruined him.

Life ruined him, Iris said. Like it ruins everyone.

Like it ruined you? Walter said.

Yes, Iris said. And you too.

Walter noticed the paleness of Eddie's skin, the blue of his lips.

I didn't care enough, he thought. He remembered the times when

Eddie was a boy and he'd ignored him, or times when he didn't feel like making dinner and Eddie ended up eating crackers or dried cereal. He wondered how many people cried at funerals because of regret, because of guilt. Most of them, I bet. Then he remembered the meanest thing of all. It had happened a few weeks after Iris's death. Eddie had told him he'd seen his mother in his dreams. He said he'd talked to her, and he asked Walter if it was really her. No, Walter had said. She's gone. He'd answered the question suddenly and without hesitation, and now he wondered why he hadn't just lied to the boy and said: Yes, that was your mother, and you can talk to her in your dreams. He was only dreaming of his mother, he thought. And you took that away from him. And yet you ended up doing the same thing and he knew it and he let you have her! You stole her and kept her all to yourself. He started to cry. Jeremy offered him a tissue.

    You're being a fool, Iris said.

    Then I've always been a fool. And now it's time to stop. Now it's time to give you back.

    Good for you, the other voice said.

    Walter knew he was right, that the voice inside him was right; he knew it had always been right. He wiped his eyes, looked down at Eddie again, and then placed the portrait in the casket, on Eddie's chest. As soon as he did this it felt as though a piece of him had been ripped out, torn away. He walked over to the far wall where he sat in one of the chairs and looked out the window, to the bridge.

    It's hard to breathe, he said.

    He waited for Iris to speak.

    She's gone, the voice told him.

    It's just a picture, he told himself.

    That's right.

    Just a picture.

    He could see the portrait in the casket from where he sat. Then his head felt light and the room began to spin.

    I'm going to throw up, he thought.

Listen to yourself, the voice said.

Walter struggled to keep from vomiting. He looked over at the casket again, and again he started to cry. Penitence, he thought. For all of it, for everything I've done or didn't do. This is how it's supposed to feel. This is how it feels to settle up.

You're doing the right thing, the voice assured him.

He leant forward in the chair, his stomach curling, knotting up.

It'll pass, the voice said.

He thought of going back home to his apartment alone.

Iris?

Just saying her name relieved him.

He could see her in the casket.

Go home, Iris said.

In the silence of the room her voice was as clear and as soothing as the night sky. But it was distant now, far away from him; no longer in him, and he did his best not to cry again.

Prin flicked her cigarette onto the wet pavement.

"I hate cigarettes," she said.

"What do you think of all that in there?" Charlie asked.

"Oh, I don't know, Charles. I'm cold. I wish I hadn't come. Does it really matter that we stay?" She shivered. "It's all such a mess. That in there didn't even feel real to me. He looked like he was asleep."

"That's how he's supposed to look."

"It's just so creepy, with the casket and all."

Ladd and Ross followed Ivan and Dmitri back over Reversing Falls and along the water. They kept their distance, parking on the side of the road when the Chrysler pulled into Wiggins Funeral Home.

"Jeremy Wiggins," Ladd said under his breath, looking over at the funeral home. "How many times have I busted that little prick for weed?"

Ross frowned.

"What's he doing in all this?"

✧

Dmitri squinted through the windshield. He was looking at Charlie.

"Isn't that the guy from this morning?"

"It is," Ivan said. "Don't say anything to him—he's not your focus."

Dmitri huffed.

"There is no focus."

"Eddie's the focus," Ivan said.

They climbed out of the car and headed across the lot.

✧

Ladd and Ross had waited on the street until Ivan and Dmitri were inside, before parking at the back, under a cluster of bare lilac trees. They watched as Charlie and Prin made their way across the lot and climbed into Charlie's car.

"You recognize him?" Ross said.

"Our mystery man from this morning," Ladd said. He snapped a few pictures then set the camera in his lap. He was thinking now. "So we've got the Ukrainians, Jeremy Wiggins, and this guy."

"All the pieces of the puzzle," Ross said. "The only one missing is Eddie."

"I think we just found him," Ladd said. He opened his door. "You stay here. Do you have a piece?"

"Not on me."

"Sit tight," Ladd said as he climbed out.

Just then his foot slipped from under him in the snow and his

arms swung out and he fell flat on the pavement.
    Ross let out a laugh.
    "You sure you don't need me?"
    Ladd swiped at the snow on his sleeve then made his way across the lot.

Jeremy stiffened and offered a nod and a courteous smile when Ivan and Dmitri entered the viewing room. These were the men from Montreal—these were Eddie's killers. He was pleased that Walter was there when they'd arrived, sitting in the chair along the far wall, and that Charlie and Prin were still outside.

Ladd entered Wiggins Funeral Home and saw the pegboard sign with Eddie's name on it. He stepped into the viewing room. Ivan and Dmitri stood in front of the casket. Walter was sitting off to the side. Jeremy frowned then smiled, trying to cover it up. Yeah you know me, you little bastard, Ladd thought. He knew by the look on Jeremy's face that something wasn't right. He drew his gun and held it at his side. In the warmth of the room a small clump of snow slid from his pant leg and onto the floor.

Ivan and Dmitri did not care about anything except to see the body, still as a statue, lying in the casket under the lights. Ivan stood with clasped hands, not awkwardly as Walter had with his toque, but stoically, professionally. He was exhausted now in the heat of the room, and he yawned at the prospect of having to drive all the way back to Montreal tonight.
    "And so here he is," he said, his hands still clasped.

Dmitri sighed heavily through his nose. Now that Eddie was in front of him it infuriated him to know that his chance was gone—that Eddie had taken it from him. He placed his hand on his gun.

"He's dead and it's clean," Ivan said. "That's all that matters."

Dmitri shook his head.

"It fuckin matters to me."

"Breathe," Ivan whispered. He turned and saw Ladd, and their eyes met.

Ross ducked below the dash when Ivan and Dmitri exited the building. He watched as they calmly made their way across the parking lot, climbed into the Chrysler and drove off. Once they were gone, he rushed across the lot and up the stairs. Ladd was standing alongside Jeremy, in front of the casket.

"The Ukrainians are gone," Ross huffed. He was bent over, trying to catch his breath. "They got away."

"That's fine," Ladd said.

"I don't understand."

"They didn't do anything."

"We're not bringing them in?"

"For what," Ladd said, "Tourism?"

Ross frowned and looked down at Eddie.

"What the hell's going on?"

Ladd grinned.

"He's asleep. They set the whole thing up—Jeremy and Eddie and our mystery man—" He flipped through his notepad. "Charlie White."

Ross was still frowning.

"But how did the Ukrainians know?"

Ladd nudged Jeremy.

"Tell him what you told me."

Jeremy's forehead shone with sweat. He loosened his tie.

◇

There'd been a fine layer of smoke hovering head-high throughout Jeremy's apartment. Charlie and Eddie were passing a joint back and forth.

"This is too fucked up," Jeremy said. "I can't believe this is happening." He went to the kitchen for another glass of juice and drank it down. "We can't stay here—we know that much. We can maybe crash at the funeral home till my parents get back—that'll buy us a few days."

"Sleep in a coffin," Eddie said.

"Yeah," Jeremy said. "Keep joking about it, man. Meanwhile, we're both dead, thanks to you." Then he froze. "Wait a second…" He skipped into his bedroom and returned with a pen and paper and cleared a space on the coffee table and started writing. Charlie and Eddie sat silent, passing the joint back and forth.

"What are you doing?" Eddie finally asked.

"Give me a minute," Jeremy said. Then he stopped and looked up. "How long did you work at Mel's?"

"Six years," Eddie said, frowning. "What does that have to do with anything?"

Jeremy put his head down and wrote a few more lines then handed the paper to Eddie, who read it aloud. They all smiled.

"My parents are away till Sunday," Jeremy said.

There was moment when nobody spoke; all of them absorbing the idea.

"They'll need to see a body," Eddie said. "They'll need to see me. I'd shit myself if they were just standing there looking at me."

"You can sleep through it," Jeremy said. "Take a roofie."

"I don't have any roofies."

"Really?"

"I don't sell date-rape pills to nobody," Eddie said.

"But you sell coke," Jeremy said.

Charlie handed Eddie the joint.

"It could work," Charlie said.

"Will you help us?" Jeremy asked.

Charlie shrugged.

"Sure, why not?"

◆

Ross peered down into the casket at Eddie. Ladd was still grinning.

"We sat down and planned the whole thing out," Jeremy said. "The wake was easy. But we needed the obit in the paper, and that required a death certificate. We couldn't do anything till we got it. Getting it in the paper was crucial."

◆

"It's laundry night," Charlie had said. "I'll see you guys tomorrow."

"Make sure you get a newspaper before you go over there," Jeremy had said. "Don't forget, man—we're counting on you."

A short while later, Jeremy and Eddie drove to the city morgue in the Wiggins company van. Jeremy went in through the rear entrance to the basement, the same way he always went.

The autopsy room was spotless. There was the chalky smell of cleanser, of shining linoleum, of the dull shine of the cement floor. Medical Examiner Dr. Edward Ramsey was standing over a cadaver and offered Jeremy a smile. He was holding a bloodied scalpel. There was a cart beside him with other bloodied tools—a bone saw, more scalpels, and a long knife. The metal and blood shone under the lights.

"You're early," Dr. Ramsey said. "This won't be ready until tomorrow."

"I need a favour," Jeremy said. "Can we talk in your office?"

Dr. Ramsey placed the scalpel on the cadaver and pulled off his gloves and escorted Jeremy into his office. His desk was meticulously clean—a file folder at one end and a framed photo of him and his wife Irene on the other. There was once a photo of him badly sunburned on a singles cruise, but now it was of him and his wife on a beach in Dominica, the day they were married. Dr. Ramsey glanced at the picture as

Jeremy sat in the chair opposite him.

"What's up?"

"I'm playing a little prank on a buddy," Jeremy said. "I need a death certificate."

Dr. Ramsey opened a drawer and pulled out a blank form and slid it across his desk. Jeremy slid it back.

"Can you fill it out? I want it to look real."

Dr. Ramsey started his computer and tapped at his keyboard.

"You didn't get this from me."

"No problem," Jeremy said.

"What's the name?"

"Edward James Smythe Jr."

"S-M-Y?"

"Yup."

Dr. Ramsey was grinning as he typed.

"A little prank, eh?"

"Yeah."

"Date of birth?"

Jeremy pulled out a piece of paper with Eddie's information.

"April 21, 1984."

"In Saint John?"

"Yup."

"Cause of death?"

"Suicide."

Dr. Ramsey looked up.

"How do you want me to say he did it?"

"I don't know," Jeremy said. "What's the best way?"

"The best way?"

"Yeah—what do you think?"

Dr. Ramsey sat back in his chair.

"What's your friend like?"

Jeremy shrugged.

"Normal guy."

"How do you think he'd do it?"
Jeremy chuckled.
"He'd never have the balls to do it."
"Okay," Dr. Ramsey said. He was typing again. "So he wouldn't use a gun—nothing too violent. How about an overdose?"
Jeremy smiled.
"Perfect."

Next they drove to the *Telegraph-Journal* building. Eddie waited outside the doors of the front reception area. Milt Landers opened the door. Milt was the Arts & Culture editor and was thin and artsy, with a trimmed beard, black rimmed glasses, cords and a sweater vest.
"What's going on, Eddie? Fancy meeting you here." It was a nervous joke and he laughed a bit too much for it. Once they were inside, Milt was no longer laughing. "Can I see it?"
Eddie dug into his pocket and pulled out the obituary.
Milt read it.
"I need the death certificate."
Eddie handed it over.
Milt was shaking his head.
"I could get in shit for this." He stood for a few seconds thinking it over. "Kurt's still here—he's down in the press room. I'll see what he can do. Have a seat—I might be a while."
Eddie sat in one of the chairs. The room was dark. He glanced over at the reception desk, at the TELEGRAPH-JOURNAL emblem on the wall, at the clock underneath it. He thought about tomorrow, about everything. And now that the coke was wearing off everything suddenly became very real to him. I could die tomorrow, he thought. He didn't think of Walter, nor of his stubbornness toward him. He didn't think of his parents or what his life might have been like had they not been killed. He didn't think what they might have thought of him now,

of what he'd become. He only thought of how this was going to end; that this absurd plan had better work or he was dead. He glanced over at the clock. Milt had been gone nearly ten minutes. What if he couldn't do it? Everything would be lost. His palms started to sweat. He wished he'd brought the coke with him; he needed another line. He stood up and paced about the room.

Then out came Milt.

"It's done."

"That still doesn't explain how the Ukrainians knew," Ross said.

"Go on," Ladd said, nudging Jeremy again.

Jeremy rolled on the balls of his feet.

"That's where Charlie came in."

Shadows moved under the bathroom door. Charlie was still thinking of Dostoevsky. Breathe. Follow the plan. It's the only way out of this. Use your head. In a flash he envisioned what he was going to do and how he was going to do it. He breathed again and stepped out into the hall. Ivan grabbed him and threw him up against the wall. Charlie felt the cold of the gun lodged against his throat, under his jaw, and he forgot everything he was going to say.

"That's not him!" Dmitri said.

Ivan, very calmly, studied Charlie's face.

"Where is he?"

"He's dead," Charlie said. He felt the gun press harder into his throat and his windpipe tightened. "He killed himself on Wednesday. He owed me money. I broke in to see if I can recoup some of my losses." He'd remembered that line and he felt he'd delivered it well and was instantly calmer now that things were falling into place. "It's in the paper—in the hall."

Ivan slipped the gun off Charlie's throat but still had him pressed against the wall. He turned to Dmitri.

"Go get it."

Dmitri went away then returned. Ivan had taken a step back from Charlie so that he was no longer in his face.

"It's in the back," Charlie said. "In the obituaries."

Dmitri fumbled with the newspaper, tossing the pages onto the floor.

"Well?" Ivan said.

Dmitri skimmed the death notices until his eyes stopped and he read for a few seconds then looked up at Ivan, stupefied. Ivan snatched the newspaper and read it himself. He turned, calmly, to Charlie.

"Get lost."

Charlie scampered out of the apartment and down the stairs.

Ross perked up.

"That was him running from the building this morning."

"Exactly," Ladd said.

"Do my parents need to know about this?" Jeremy said. "I didn't know what else to do. You gotta believe me."

"Forget it, kid," Ladd said. "When Eddie wakes up, tell him I'll be in touch."

When he and Ross climbed into their car, they both sighed, looking over at the funeral home.

"It can't be that easy," Ross said.

Ladd shrugged.

"He looked pretty dead to me."

Ross reached into the backseat for the newspaper he'd brought with him in the morning. He flipped through it and found the death notices.

"Well I'll be damned."

"*He had a passion for footwear!*" Ladd read and laughed.

Ross straightened himself in his seat.

"So the Ukrainians waited out the day to confirm everything at the wake."

Ladd was still laughing.

"They're clever little buggers, I'll give them that."

Chapter 16

April was curled up on her couch watching *Law & Order* when Charlie and Prin showed up at her door.

"She's asleep," she said softly. "I can wake her."

"No," Prin said. "I just want to see her."

They cracked open the bedroom door as the light shone on Daisy, a mess of hair over her face, a few of her dolls strewn about the bed. Charlie looked over Prin's shoulder. It was like looking at a fine piece of art; he had no words but to only stare in silence.

"She's so beautiful," he finally whispered.

"Isn't she?" Prin said.

"I can't believe I made her."

Prin smiled.

"I say that sometimes too."

April was smoking a cigarette.

"She was great—went down without a peep."

"I don't know what I'd do without you," Prin said.

April waved the compliment away and smoked.

"She's easy—you know that." She leaned over and butted her cigarette in the ashtray beside her on the couch. "Where are you two off to now?"

"We're heading over to his place," Prin said.

Charlie shrugged.

"Nightcap."

April lit another cigarette and scampered into the kitchen.

"I almost forgot—I grabbed this for you." She handed Prin the sheet of paper from the Laundromat. Prin folded it and placed it in her pocket.

They stopped at the liquor store for a twelve-pack of Corona. They carried blankets and two lawn chairs up to the roof. There was a layer of crusted snow and Charlie took the beers out of the case and twisted them into the snow. They wrapped themselves in the blankets and looked out over the rooftops. The sky was so dark they could not see where it met the water, just the lights of the toll bridge and the port. Prin blew into the cold air, watching her breath.

"It's so nice up here, even in the winter," she said.

Charlie drank his beer.

"What if I'm no good at it?"

"At what?" Prin frowned.

"Being a father."

"It's easy, Charles—all you have to do is con her with Kinder Eggs."

Charlie chuckled.

Prin tucked her chin under the blanket.

"You won't leave her, will you Charles? I can't have you come into her life then leave."

"You left before," Charlie said. "Not me."

"I know—but that was different. We were both different then— everything was different."

Charlie looked out to the bay.

"I've never been good at anything."

"Oh stop feeling sorry for yourself," Prin said. "It's okay to be scared, but there's no cowering with this."

"Then why do you cower with me?" Charlie said. "We're good together—you know that. And think about Daisy—wouldn't it be nice to give her a stable home?"

"I give her a stable home," Prin said.

"I mean with a dad too," Charlie said. "Two normal parents. That can't be a bad thing, can it?"

Prin pulled out the piece of paper April had given her.

Charlie lit a joint.

"Let me see that," he said. Prin handed it to him and he read it. "This is good—no?"

"I'm scared too, Charles. I make good money doing what I do. It's okay to sacrifice for my child."

"Not that kind of sacrifice," Charlie said. He held up the paper. "This would be good—you'd be good at this."

"Do you really love me, Charles?"

"I do."

There were tears on Prin's cheeks, half frozen.

"Why?"

"I don't know," Charlie said. "I just do—isn't that enough? Why do you love me?"

Prin crossed her arms, tightening the blanket around her.

"You don't see through me," she said.

A siren whirled in the distance.

"There are rules with Daisy," she said. "It's not all fun and games. You can't drink and drive with her in the car—I won't have it."

Charlie took a final haul on the joint, flicked it into the snow, watched it fizzle out, then chugged the rest of his beer and reached down for another.

"Okay," he said.

"I mean it."

"I promise."

"And of course there will be other things," Prin said. "I just can't think of them right now."

"Let's get married," Charlie said. "You'd make a good nagging wife."

Prin chuckled.

"I'm serious," Charlie said. "We'll go to City Hall first thing in the morning."

"Slow down, Charles."

Charlie watched his breath in the frosty air.

"Do you know that big house I took you to today?" He picked a bottle cap from the snow and flicked it over the ledge. "I've always had this weird fantasy that I lived there; that somehow that'd make me happy. Up until now I've always believed that." He sighed heavily, the kind of sigh that comes before an admission. "The truth is, I just don't want to be alone anymore."

"Who does?" Prin said.

A wind blew across the rooftop. Flecks of snow tickled their eyes.

"It's been a long winter," she said. "I miss summer."

Charlie smiled.

"Me too."

Chapter 17

Walter walked home from Wiggins Funeral Home; he'd gone the length of Chesley Drive along the water—roughly a half-hour—without looking over at the toll bridge. He didn't want to see it; he'd always felt, in some small way, that it had belonged to him, but now it belonged to everyone. It has always belonged to everyone, he thought. Just as Iris has always belonged to Eddie. It pained him to admit this, and he didn't want to think about anything anymore, and for the first time in as long as he could remember, it was easy to do that; there were no voices, just the scrunching of the snow under his feet. As he approached Reversing Falls Bridge he looked over at his building, at the darkened windows, and he felt the emptiness of it and wondered if anyone had ever looked at it and felt the same way. I doubt it, he thought, waiting for a voice to come, expecting one, but none came.

When he got home he sat in the dark, still in his winter jacket. He listened as the traffic passed, their lights swooning across the walls. Okay then, he thought. It's just me. This is how it's supposed to be. He tried to think of the sound of Iris's voice but he couldn't and he knew then how far away from him she now was. He remembered feeling this way when she'd died; that she'd gone away from him and there was no getting her back. And now Eddie too, he thought, and although it had been years since he'd heard his voice, now that he was gone he longed for it. He sat like this, in the dark, his gut full of regret and guilt, for an hour, before his buzzer rang.

He made his way downstairs and opened the door and there before him, in the flesh, was Eddie, the portrait of Iris in his hand; two ghosts in his doorway. Jeremy was standing behind him. Walter stammered back and Eddie caught him and sat beside him on the stairs.

"Easy now, Walt—I'm here—right here."

"I don't understand," Walter said.

"It wasn't real," Eddie said. He peered down at the portrait. "When I woke up with this on my chest I knew it was you."

"So you're not dead?" Walter said.

Eddie smiled.

"No."

Walter motioned to the portrait.

"And Iris?"

"Iris what?" Eddie said.

"She's not dead either?"

Eddie stood up, and with a sad smile, offered his hand.

"Come on, Walt, let's get you upstairs."

Walter's legs were still shaky when they got up to his apartment. He flicked on the lights and went to the fridge, got three cans of Alpine and handed them out. Eddie and Jeremy explained everything.

"I figured the best place to hide was out in the open," Eddie said. "You taught me that."

Walter grinned, remembering their games of hide-and-seek when Eddie was a boy. But looking at Eddie now, he was reminded of just how much time had passed.

"I didn't expect you to come," Eddie said. "I didn't think you'd find out."

"I saw it in the paper," Walter said. He took a moment, absorbing everything he'd been told; hitmen, drug deals—none of it sounded real.

"I'm sorry you had to see that," Eddie said.

"I've missed you, Eddie."

Eddie finished his beer then patted Walter's knee and stood up.

"I'm tired—it's been a crazy day."

"Tomorrow morning," Walter said. "Tim's at Lancaster Mall—coffee?"

"Sure," Eddie said.

Walter wrapped his arms around him. Eddie stood stiffly and patted him on the back. Walter gripped him hard, long enough to make Eddie smile.

"Okay then," Walter said. "Tomorrow then."

He closed the door behind them. The first thing he saw was Iris, perched on the coffee table.

You've not lost him after all, she said.

Walter went to the fridge for another beer.

What are you going to say to him?

I don't know. Anything. Everything.

Where do you start?

With coffee, Walter said.

This is all so exciting! Iris said. Isn't it?

Chapter 18

By the time Jeremy and Eddie got to Eddie's apartment, Eddie's head was clearing up. As soon as he opened his door and stepped inside he put out his arms and smiled wide. "Home sweet home," he said. He put on a Strokes cd and turned it up loud. The drumbeat pounded, the music upbeat and celebratory and he danced about the room. He leaned over the coffee table, cut two lines of coke, snorted then sat up, re-energized. His apartment was smaller than Jeremy's, but equally messy; a dingy couch and a cluttered coffee table and bare walls except for a poster of a bikini-clad Kate Upton above the TV. He filled two glasses with scotch and handed one to Jeremy.

"Cheers, man, to us—for actually pulling this off."

Their glasses clinked and they drank.

Eddie started rolling a joint.

Jeremy pulled a small block of hash from his pocket.

"Where's your pipe?"

Eddie examined the coffee table.

"Check the kitchen."

Jeremy searched the kitchen, through the clutter on the table and the counter.

"So who else came to my wake?" Eddie asked.

"Charlie was there, with a chick."

"That's it?"

"That's it," Jeremy said. He started opening cupboards.

Eddie lit the joint.

"Try my room."

Jeremy went into the bedroom and rummaged through the end table drawers. He lifted and shook the bed sheets, then stood, arms crossed, and sighed. "IT'S NOT HERE," he said, his voice raised over the music. Then he knelt down and looked under the bed and there it was. He dropped down onto his belly and stretched, his fingers nicking it. He made himself as flat as he could and stretched further, nicking it again. Then he got up, pushed the bed a little to the side, lay on his belly again, and finally got it. He went back into the living room.

The music was blaring.

The apartment door was open.

Eddie was flopped over on the couch, his eyes open and blank, a hole in his forehead, another in his chest, the joint smoldering between his fingers.

Dmitri unscrewed the silencer and placed his gun in the glove box. He was licking his lips as the Chrysler made its way swiftly down Carmarthen Street and around Lower Cove Loop.

"I fuckin smoked him!"

"You did," Ivan said. He was steady at the wheel. He did not look at the buildings along Water Street, not even while they were stopped at a red light.

"How did you know?" Dmitri asked.

Ivan yawned; a long, drawn-out yawn that made his eyes water.

"A hunch," he said. He was too tired to explain how he'd suspected something was amiss from the start; that he'd seen Ladd and Ross outside Eddie's apartment at the same time Ladd had spotted them; and that he'd known all day that they were being followed; that he'd seen Ladd and his bright red hair and his camera too many times; that he'd toured the city hoping they'd lose interest; that he'd seen Eddie breathing as he lay in the casket, the picture on his chest moving with each breath; and finally, that if they waited outside Eddie's building long enough, Eddie would show up, and sure enough, he did. He yawned again. He'd tell him another time. But not now. Now all he wanted to do was settle in and drive.

They crossed the overpass and turned onto the highway and headed across the toll bridge, over the harbour. Dmitri had taken off his jacket and tossed it into the backseat. He'd stopped licking his lips.

"You okay?" Ivan asked.

"He just sat there."

"That's how it goes sometimes."

"He didn't even have time to react."

"No, he didn't," Ivan said.

The Chrysler slowed as they passed through the open tolls.

"It didn't feel like anything," Dmitri said.

"Don't think about it."

The Chrysler accelerated. Dmitri looked out his window, to the restaurant at Reversing Falls and the stacks of the pulp mill on the other side of the bridge.

"I did good, though, right?—clean and done?"

Ivan lit a cigarette. The lights of the city were in his rear view mirror.

"Clean and done," he said. But in his head he knew they weren't in the clear just yet.

Two police cars, a fire truck, and an ambulance had rushed to the scene, lighting up the block along Carmarthen Street, the blue and red lights blinking off the buildings. A few people were milling around on the sidewalk. Others watched from their windows. Jeremy was in the hall with an officer when Detective Ladd arrived. He knew what had happened as soon as the call came through. He slipped around a technician who was dusting the doorframe for fingerprints, and stepped inside. A woman stood over the body, snapping photos. She glanced over at Ladd then without expression, went back to work. The lights from outside flashed and blinked on the walls. Ladd sighed. He'd had them. He remembered what Ross had said—that it couldn't be that easy. He stepped back into the hall.

"Get this out right away—we're looking for a black, late model Chrysler 300, heading west, Quebec plates…" He pulled out his notepad and flipped through the pages. "453 MVJ. Two men. Ukrainian. Call Fredericton RCMP. Tell them to be ready. The border too."

The officer rushed down the stairs.

"Did you see them?" Ladd asked.

Jeremy shook his head. His eyes were glossy, his hands shaking. Ladd took him by the shoulders.

"I need you to focus for a second. Can you do that?"

Jeremy nodded and blinked. Then he heaved and lurched forward, and vomited at Ladd's feet.

"How long ago were they here?" Ladd asked, unfazed.

Jeremy wiped his mouth on his sleeve.

"Concentrate," Ladd said.

"I don't know," Jeremy said. "Twenty minutes maybe. I called 911 as soon as it happened." He turned quickly, facing the wall, then bent over and vomited again.

Ladd rushed downstairs and jumped into his car and sped off.

Chapter 19

Ivan's eyes were heavy as they pushed on through Welsford, a sparse rural community carved out of the forest and hills north of Grand Bay. He lit a cigarette. It was a clear night and the highway was white with salt. He regretted not taking out Jeremy too. Clean and done. But at the time he was more concerned with Dmitri. And he'd done well; a perfect shot, straight to the heart. One more, Ivan had said. Dmitri took a step toward Eddie and put one in his forehead and they left. But now that it was over Ivan was able to reflect, and he was angered at himself for the mistake, for not taking out Jeremy too and avoiding the situation he figured they were now in. The Chrysler accelerated. Montreal felt a million miles away. It wasn't long after this when the lights appeared in his mirror.

Dmitri perked up when he saw the lights. Ivan nodded to the dash. Dmitri grabbed the guns, his eyes popping out of his head.

"Stay calm," Ivan said. He flicked his signal and slowed to a stop along a patch of highway with trees on both sides of the road.

The patrol car stopped behind them. Ivan watched in his mirror as two officers approached, guns drawn. The lights flashed and blinked on the trees.

Ivan motioned with his hand for Dmitri to keep his gun low.

The officer on Dmitri's side struggled in the snowbank.

"SHOW ME YOUR HANDS!" the officer on Ivan's side shouted.

Ivan cracked his window.

"HANDS!" the officer repeated.

"What's the problem?"

"HANDS—NOW!"

Ivan cracked the window a little more and waved his fingers.

"Okay, okay, relax."

The officer took a step closer, nearly beside the car door.

"SHOW ME YOUR HANDS—"

Two quick bursts from Ivan's gun shattered the window and the officer fell back onto the road. Ivan slammed the car into Drive and spun away as the second officer fired into the rear window and Dmitri fired back and the officer dropped behind the snowbank.

The highway wound through the trees. Ivan drove as fast he could, looking for a side road, anything off the highway. Every set of headlights made him tense. He kept his eyes on the road, and it was only when Dmitri coughed and blood spewed onto the dash that he realized Dmitri had been shot. He reached across the seat. Blood filled Dmitri's shirt and he coughed again, cringing, the blood running down his chin, his eyes watering.

On the outskirts of Welsford they came around a bend and there, set high in the middle of a field, was an old farmhouse sheltered by a cluster of trees. Ivan pulled into the driveway which was neatly plowed and rose steadily up the field to the house. Behind it was a huge weathered barn, its tin roof silvery blue in the moonlight.

Inside the house, Joseph and Enid Tierney were in the kitchen. Joseph was half-asleep on the cot near the front window. Enid had just dried the last dish and was now sitting, as she always did, on the oven door, taking in the heat from the wood-burning stove attached to it. The kitchen still smelled of pork chops and onions. Enid's shirt was starting to feel hot, just the way she liked it, warming her skin, when she saw the lights coming up the driveway.

"Joe," she said. "Someone's here."

Joseph lifted his old frame from off the cot and put on his barn coat and boots. "Someone probably wantin eggs," he said. He went to the back room and returned with an armload of wood and dropped it into the box beside the stove. The Chrysler pulled up near the house and stopped for a moment before parking by the barn. Joseph stepped outside, felt the cold, tucked his chin into the front of his coat, and made his way across the yard. The car's rear window was shattered, as was the driver's window. Ivan stepped out. Bits of glass spilled onto the ground.

"Help me," he said, shuffling around to the passenger side and opening the door. Dmitri, barely conscious, was slumped in the seat. Joseph still hadn't spoken.

"We've had an accident," Ivan said.

Joseph saw the blood on Dmitri's shirt.

"I'll call an ambulance."

"You will not," Ivan said. He held his gun low. "Help me get him inside."

Joseph glanced back to the house. Ivan saw Enid at the window.

"What do you want?" Joseph asked.

"Your help," Ivan said, holding up Dmitri.

Joseph grabbed Dmitri by the arm and they dragged him across the yard and into the house and placed him on the cot. Enid was standing, mouth agape.

"Get some towels," Joseph said.

"What happened?"

"Towels, Edie!"

"I'm calling 911," Enid said.

Ivan pulled out his gun. He did not point it.

Enid's eyes widened and she stepped back and braced herself against the kitchen table. She could hear the hockey game in the back room. Ivan did too.

"Who else is here?"

"Our grandson," Joseph said. "He's just a lad."

"Leave him be."

Dmitri groaned and coughed more blood.

"Towels," Ivan said to Enid. "And no funny stuff." He placed his gun back in his pocket and turned to Joseph. "Put the car in the barn."

And if you try anything—"

"Easy now," Joseph said, raising his hands. "You got nothin to worry about from us."

"Do you have guns in this house?"

"I got a 12-gauge and a .30-30."

"You do what you're told and you'll be fine," Ivan said.

Joseph stepped outside. Ivan watched through the window as the old man slid open the big barn door, backed out a red Ford half-ton and pulled the Chrysler inside and closed the door again.

Enid returned with an armful of towels. Ivan ripped off Dmitri's shirt and wiped away the blood that poured from the wound which was about the size of a dime. He pressed the towel to it, but the towel seemed to absorb more blood than stop any bleeding. Enid took her place beside the kitchen table. Joseph came back inside and stood beside her.

"How much gas is in the truck?" Ivan asked.

"Oh, about half a tank," Joseph said, casually enough for Ivan to notice. "But I got a diesel pump in the barn."

"Take me to the guns."

Joseph led Ivan through the back room where their grandson, Kevin, was laying on the couch watching a hockey game, then to the back of the house where he slid open two doors and stepped into a cold and musty den. Joseph plopped into the chair behind a solid oak desk. Ivan noted that this old man was not afraid of him, how he'd plopped into the chair, more tired than afraid. He was a smart old man; he knew Ivan spoke the truth when he said he wouldn't hurt them. Lining the wall beside the desk was a huge glass case housing the shotgun and the rifle, a set of antlers, and a framed picture of a young soldier with a military medal next to it. Ivan had noticed this same picture on the windowsill in the kitchen. Joseph saw him looking at it.

"My son," he said. "Kevin's father."

"Is he coming tonight?" Ivan asked.

Joseph shook his head and stared blankly at the picture.

"He passed four years ago."

There was a sudden, cold silence in the room. Ivan felt guilty for what he was doing; he wasn't a home invader, especially to people like this, and the whole thing made him uneasy.

"Does the boy live with you?"

Joseph shook his head.

"Kevin's mother's pickin him up in the mornin." He noticed Ivan's eyes widen. "She won't do you no harm." He slid open a desk drawer, took a key and opened the case and stepped back. "Take what you need. The .30-30 shoots straight."

Ivan grabbed the shotgun and the rifle, a box of shells and a box of cartridges. When they returned to the kitchen Enid was still standing beside the table. Ivan sat at the end of the cot. He knew Enid would do exactly what he said; that his presence was traumatic enough to cement her in place.

The towel on Dmitri's stomach was soaked through with blood. Ivan replaced it with another, tucking the bloodied one under the cot.

Then the boy, Kevin, sauntered into the kitchen. He was in his pajamas, a scrawny kid, his hair matted. He went to the fridge, snatched a juice box, poked the straw, sipped and left without looking at anyone.

"He's just a boy," Enid said timidly.

"I'm not going to hurt anyone," Ivan said, softly, realizing how his tone had changed since coming from the den.

Dmitri grunted.

"He's likely bleedin pretty good on the inside too," Joseph said.

Ivan pressed the towel against the wound and Dmitri grunted again, then opened his eyes.

"Thirsty."

"Some water," Ivan said.

Enid, moving away from the kitchen table for the first time since she'd gotten the towels, went to the sink and filled a glass with water. Ivan held it to Dmitri's lips. A trickle of water spilled down Dmitri's chin. His eyes were red and frightened. Ivan was beyond tired now, but he'd expected to be awake all night anyway and he reminded himself of this.

He turned to Enid again.

"Make me a pot of coffee," he said. "Please."

In the distance, the sound of sirens then the passing lights on the highway below. Ivan tipped the glass to Dmitri's lips again. His mind swirled. Dmitri was bleeding to death before his eyes, and for the first time in his life he didn't know what to do. He lit a cigarette. Enid turned and glared at him, then faced the counter again, watching the coffee percolating. She huffed before going into the back room.

"Kevin has asthma," Joseph whispered.

Ivan smoked. Enid returned. Ivan took another puff. Then he got to his feet and went to the front porch. He'd almost chuckled to himself as he smoked, his nerves twitching in his veins; rudeness was the least of his worries. When he came back inside, a mug of coffee, a cup of sugar, and a jug of milk sat on the kitchen table. Joseph was sipping his own coffee. Ivan noticed that Enid was no longer in the kitchen.

"She's puttin Kevin to bed," Joseph said. He grinned. "You done right doin that—goin outside. You would'a had a real problem if you didn't."

Ivan gave a tiny grin. Dmitri grunted and coughed up more blood.

"I could take him to the outdoor," Joseph said. "You go on with the truck and I'll take your car."

Ivan frowned.

"The outdoor?"

"The hospital," Joseph said.

Ivan shook his head. He poured the milk into his coffee. Joseph saw him looking at the milk, sniffing the jug, and he smiled.

"Straight from the cow," he said. "I bet you ain't never had that before."

Ivan sniffed his coffee before stirring it. The thought of taking the truck had crossed his mind, but there was no way he was going anywhere tonight. They would leave in the morning, and he would take Joseph's truck; that much he'd figured out. Snow blew across the field and brushed against the windows. Joseph dropped another log into the stove. More sirens and more lights passed on the highway below.

◇

Ladd flew past the cars on the highway, siren blaring, lights flashing. If he could get to them somewhere between Fredericton and Woodstock, there really was no place for them to go other than the highway; there was nothing but forest and hills and the St. John River. He'd received a call about the plates; they'd been stolen from a Ford Taurus in Laval, Quebec, a year ago. He wasn't surprised. But whoever plates they were, those were still the plates on the Chrysler 300 they were looking for.

When he got to Welsford he reduced his speed; the highway went to single lanes and twisted and turned through a few sparse communities. As he rounded a corner the forest was lit up by a team of cruisers and two fire trucks. A body lay on the road, covered with a tarp. Firefighters were in the snowbank, working on someone else. Ladd pulled over just as the ambulance arrived. He flashed his badge at a detective standing next to the abandoned cruiser.

"Any witnesses?"

The detective shook his head.

"You'll be looking for a black Chrysler 300," Ladd said. "Two men."

The detective looked at Ladd.

"We figured that. APB came in a while back."

"How long ago did they come through?" Ladd asked.

"About a half-hour," the detective said. "They ran the plates, pulled them over, approached, shots fired." He nodded to the body in the road. "Two in the chest, point blank." In the snowbank, paramedics were escorting the other officer into the ambulance. "One grazed the side of his face—took a chunk of ear. One more in the shoulder."

"I know this isn't my jurisdiction" Ladd said. "But I want these assholes just as bad as you do. What can I do to help?"

"We've got roadblocks in Oromocto and Fredericton," the detective said. "House-to-house search just started here in Welsford. But for all we know they could be in Fredericton by now. If that's the case, they could be anywhere."

"I can go house-to-house," Ladd said.

"Appreciate that," the detective said. "Go on up the road a ways and you'll find our boys. I'll let 'em know you're coming."

Chapter 20

Ivan sat facing the window. He'd drunk two cups of coffee and was no longer tired, the caffeine tingling through his body. The wind had picked up, blowing across the field in gusts. It had been a while since any police cars had passed on the highway. Beyond the highway the forest was black and endless and Ivan wondered if it weren't for the cold they could head into the woods and hide there. But the weather wasn't the problem; Dmitri hadn't moved much since he was placed on the cot, and more importantly, the towels hadn't stopped the bleeding.

Joseph remained at the kitchen table. He too had drunk two cups of coffee. He'd gotten some biscuits from the breadbox and they'd eaten them with butter and jam. Enid had gone to bed. She'd lain awake for an hour before she fell asleep, listening to Joseph and Ivan talking in the kitchen below.

Then a set of headlights turned into the driveway and headed up to the house. It took all of Ivan's strength to lift Dmitri off the cot and get him to the couch in the back room. He could see the headlights approaching, between the snowbanks and around the side of the house to the yard. He slid the rifle under the cot, loaded the shotgun and stood just beyond the entrance to the back room. He could see Ladd through the window, that bright red hair, looking at the barn. He knew if Ladd looked down he'd see the bits of glass under his feet, the drops of blood leading into the house.

Joseph turned on the yard light and stepped out to the front porch. Ivan listened from the doorway.

Ladd flashed his badge.

"Sorry to bother you. We're looking for two men on the run. Have you seen anyone around your property tonight?"

Joseph peered out to the barn.

"Not tonight. I suppose you'd see their tracks in the field if they came this way. You can go have a look if you want."

Ladd turned and looked down over the field to the highway.

"No, that's fine."

"What'd they do?" Joseph asked.

Ivan held the shotgun to his hip, his hand on the trigger.

"They're wanted for murder," Ladd said.

The old man grunted.

"That ain't good."

"Lock your door," Ladd said. "Call 911 if you see anything."

"Okay then," Joseph said. "You take care."

Ivan ducked as the lights flashed across the wall, the cruiser slowly making its way down the driveway. Joseph sat at the kitchen table again. He didn't say anything when Ivan emptied the shotgun shells onto the floor then perched the gun against the table. The silence that had hovered over them in the den now surfaced again, simmering in the hard kitchen light.

"You wouldn't understand," Ivan finally said.

Joseph leaned forward, his elbows on the table.

"Last spring we were cullin chickens out behind the barn," he said. "Kevin came out to watch—to see us cuttin the heads off with an axe and them dancin around headless. He said to me: Grampy, why are you killin the chickens? And I said: This is a farm, and that's what farms do." He took a moment, staring across the room. "A man's business is his own business—I understand that." He was looking at his son's picture on the wall.

"How did he die?" Ivan asked.

"Accident," Joseph said. He paused, and again the silence

hovered over them. "In Gagetown. He done two tours in Afghanistan, but a blown tire on a dirt road a half-hour from home killed him. He wasn't buckled in—thrown clear out." He was still looking at the picture. "Army said he hadn't followed protocol. Sent us a big bunch of papers explainin it. I wasn't lookin to blame anyone. But they blamed him and never looked back." He sighed heavily. "It ain't easy bein a father. You don't stop worryin. I got two daughters too. One's in Korea teachin English. The other's a bigshot lawyer in Toronto."

"I could probably use a good lawyer," Ivan said, and he and Joseph shared a smile. He thought of Dmitri bleeding to death in the next room, which quickly broke his smile. He got up and checked on him and replaced the bloodied towel. Dmitri was shivering. "He needs a blanket," Ivan said.

Joseph moved stiffly through the room, his old joints cracking as he climbed the stairs to the second floor then returned a minute later with two heavy quilts. They were neatly folded and smelled of fabric softener. Ivan spread them over Dmitri. The one quilt had farm animals; cows and chickens and sheep intricately stitched into each square, and the other, covered bridges. It was the innocence of these images that made Ivan feel guilty again. When he went back into the kitchen there was a blueberry cake on the table, along with two plates. Joseph cut a slice and slid it toward him. Jesus Christ, Ivan thought. He did not understand the generosity ingrained in rural New Brunswickers; their inability to make anyone feel unwelcome; that if someone was in your home, regardless of the circumstances, you fed them. He nodded his thanks and they ate without speaking, sharing the stillness of the room, the kind of stillness that comes in the middle of the night.

"I had a son too," Ivan finally said. He wasn't sure if he should go on, but Joseph looked at him for more. He waited a moment before he spoke again. "Doctors said my wife—it would be impossible to conceive. But my wife, she's a great believer in God; she believes in miracles. She wouldn't give up. And then she got pregnant." He sighed, a long sigh; he'd said too much, he knew, but there was something between him and

Joseph now, in the stillness of the kitchen, and despite everything else that was going on, he felt a kinship with the old man. "But it wasn't meant to be. She delivered a boy. My son. Stillborn." He sighed again. "We had a funeral. His coffin. It was like that of a doll." He stared blankly, beyond Joseph. "My wife, she said he was a miracle."

"You think he was?" Joseph asked.

Ivan shook his head.

"I've seen too many things to believe such things exist."

Joseph finished his cake, scraping his fork along the plate for the crumbs.

"There's too much of that in the world these days."

"Too much of what?"

"Godlessness," Joseph said. "Is the lad the same way?"

"He's too young to know what to believe in," Ivan said.

"I'll pray for you," Joseph said. "And the lad too."

"Do you believe your boy is in heaven?" Ivan asked.

"I do," Joseph said.

"Why?"

"Because I don't want to believe that he ain't."

"Because you can't face it?"

"Face what?" Joseph frowned.

"The truth," Ivan said.

Joseph adjusted himself in his seat, sitting up straight.

"That's your truth," he said. "It ain't mine. I'm smart enough to know that I don't got all the answers and if there's a chance he's in a better place then by god that's what I believe and that's where he is."

"Fair enough," Ivan said.

"Just because something ain't in front of you don't mean it don't exist," Joseph said. He went over to the window and looked down to the highway.

Ivan could see that he was agitated.

"Why aren't you afraid of me?"

"I'm an old man," Joseph said. "Nothin scares me too much

anymore." He was still looking out the window. "And because I know deep down you're a good man."

Ivan grinned.

"I can assure you, Joseph, I'm not. But my wife, she's good to the bone—it's a miracle she's stayed with me all these years."

Joseph turned and smiled so that his whole face wrinkled up.

"There you go! You do believe in miracles!"

Ivan grinned again.

"Maybe just one."

Joseph nodded to the back room.

"So the lad, he's like your son then, ain't he?"

Ivan slid the cake dish toward him and cut another piece.

"It's complicated," he said. "I've known him since he was a boy. If anything was going to happen it would have happened by now."

"I reckon you can't force too much of anythin in this world," Joseph said.

In the morning the sun rose over the hills, over the trees that had looked so black during the night. Ivan had drunk more coffee and had smoked the last of his cigarettes. His legs were numb from sitting. Joseph had slept on the cot but he'd awoken before Ivan and had gone outside and filled the truck with fuel. He gave Ivan his barn coat and his wool cap. Ivan placed the guns in the front seat then went into the barn, where in the Chrysler's trunk was a jug of bleach. He wiped the car down; the door handles, steering wheel, the dash; everything he could soak, everywhere his fingerprints may have been. He went back into the house, put the bloodied towels in a garbage bag and threw them in the truck. He wiped down the kitchen table and chair, even the dishes he'd used. Then, when everything was done, he made his way to the back room. Each time he'd checked on Dmitri during the night he'd half expected the worst; Dmitri had lost too much blood; too many towels had been used. But Dmitri's eyes would open, he'd drink some water then close his eyes again. But now his eyes didn't open, and there was a stillness, an absence.

"Help me get him in the truck," Ivan said.

They carried Dmitri outside and gently placed him in the front seat. Joseph went inside and returned with the quilts and wrapped them around him before he clicked the seatbelt in place.

"I don't think he's breathin," Joseph said. "He ain't—"

"I know," Ivan said.

"I'm sorry," Joseph said.

Ivan shook Joseph's hand and climbed into the truck.

"So am I."

Chapter 21

Walter slept until eight o'clock in the morning, until the sunlight shone on the wall and warmed the room. There was nothing better than the warmth of the sun and it made him smile as he lay, thinking of today, his first day of retirement, his first day with Eddie again. It's a new beginning, he thought. What perfect timing. I can spend as much time with him as I like.

There, do you see? Iris said. Everything turned out as I said it would.

Walter stretched in bed, absorbing this new beginning and the feeling it gave him; a feeling of happiness, a rumbling in his belly. Jack had always talked of the rumbling, saying it came every Friday after his shift when he thought about the night ahead, and now Walter understood it.

He took a piss then, instinctively, went to put on his uniform but stopped. He grinned. What had felt sacred yesterday—putting it on for the last time—now felt insignificant. Instead, he dressed in a sweatshirt and jeans and went into the kitchen. The sky was a lovely, pure blue. The harbour sparkled. He boiled some water for coffee then went downstairs for the newspaper. He read it through, including the obituaries, and he chuckled to himself.

It's nothing to laugh about, Iris said.

He's a grown man, Walter said. Obviously he can take care of himself.

He's a drug dealer. That's what happens when a child loses his mother.

That wasn't your fault, Walter said. I was the one who let him down. I'm the reason he turned out that way.

Are you going to talk to him about it?

I don't know, Walter said. I'm just happy. I've been given a second chance and I'm not going to waste it. I don't want to push him away again.

Please talk to him, Iris said. For me.

Okay, Walter said. But not right away. He sighed and rubbed his hands together. Let's buy some more wine tonight, and maybe we could go out to eat.

I like the new you! Iris said.

I'm not done yet, Walter said.

He put on his boots and jacket and walked to the bus stop. A cold wind blew along the street but with the sun shining Walter felt like a new man in a new world. Everything seemed vibrant. The buildings, the street signs, even the stop sign looked extra red. He took the bus to the east side, to McAllister Place, and went into Sears, to the men's department, where he bought a pair of khakis, a pair of black shoes, and two wool sweaters—one bright red, the other a multicolored pattern.

When he got back to his apartment he showered, shaved, cut the tags off the khakis and multicolored sweater, tucked Iris into the front of his jacket and out he went. Lancaster Mall was a twenty-minute walk. When he got to Tim Horton's he ordered his usual, a Double-Double, and sat at a table near the window. His ankles were a little sore from his new shoes, but they were nice shoes, and he took a napkin and wiped the salt that had gathered on the toes. There'd been no other voice but Iris's since last night, since she'd come back to him, since Eddie had come back, and he was content; it felt okay now to be doing what he did, to be pretending; it felt okay admitting to himself that none of it was real. It makes you feel good, he thought. And that's real. And so is Eddie and the chance he's given you. He waited for that other voice, knowing it was there, somewhere, but it too seemed content, and remained silent. Walter liked the smell of his new clothes. He liked how he looked. He sipped on his coffee and read the news as it appeared on one of the overhead monitors; BREAKING NEWS: RCMP OFFICER KILLED, MANHUNT UNDERWAY IN FREDERICTON. Walter sipped his coffee and looked at his watch. Outside, the sun was shining.

Chapter 22

Ivan turned off the highway and headed into deeper wooded country. The sun shone brightly over the trees, the snow smooth over the ditch. The shotgun and rifle sat on the seat next to him, along with the boxes of shells and cartridges. He could smell the bleach on his hands, and the smell of the truck; of Joseph's farm; dust and hay and cobwebs and manure. But it was a good truck, and it drove smooth, and with a full tank of diesel he figured he could drive for six or seven hours without stopping. Dmitri's head was slumped back, as though he were asleep, and Ivan could not look at him.

Ladd been checking houses all night and the last of his energy was fading fast. They've made it to Fredericton, he thought, a feeling of defeat swooning over him. His cellphone rang. It was Detective Ross. He suspected the same thing. Come on home, Ross had said in a fatherly tone. Get some sleep. Let the Fredericton boys do their job. Ladd had expected Ross to give him an I-told-you-so but there was no need; his fatherly tone had said it all. Ladd cracked open his window. The fresh air awoke him a little. Then, with the gloom of defeat sinking in, he came over the crest of a hill and met a half-ton truck and caught eyes with the driver, those piercing wolf-like eyes.

The sun was in Ivan's eyes as he came over the hill and passed the unmarked cruiser. He recognized Ladd right away. He watched in his mirror as the cruiser disappeared down the hill, not sure if Ladd had made him or not. He accelerated, the road climbing and dipping and winding through the trees. Then, as he came along a stretch of road with fields on both sides, the lights appeared in the mirror. He gripped the wheel tight as the truck picked up speed, the engine humming, distancing himself from the lights behind him. Toward the end of the clearing a whitetail deer appeared at the edge of the road. It perked its head up and leapt across the road. Ivan had been looking in the mirror and he saw the deer at the last second and jerked the wheel and the truck spun and slammed through the snow and jumped clear of the ditch and stopped thirty yards off the road. The deer bounded in and out of the snow and disappeared gracefully into the treeline. Ivan had smashed his nose on the steering wheel and blood poured over his mouth and chin. Dazed, he fumbled through the cab, gathering the shells and cartridges from off the floor. Dmitri's seatbelt had kept him in place, his head slumped forward. The cruiser stopped near the ditch, at the end of the path the truck had made in the snow.

Ivan ducked low and sprawled across the seat, his legs over Dmitri's lap. He opened the truck's door just enough to squeeze the end of the rifle through. He eyed the cruiser through the sight and fired four shots into the windshield.

Ladd was already outside, tucked behind the front wheel-well. He poked his head out and returned fire, the bullets ricocheting off the truck, whizzing through the cab.

Ivan dropped his head and fired back, the bullets plunking into the cruiser's hood and grill, the crack of the rifle echoing through the hills. He could see his breath as he peeked through the slit in the open door. His eyes were starting to swell, his nose throbbing, pulsing blood. He reloaded the .30-30 and fired again. Ladd hadn't returned fire. Ivan waited, looking for movement. There was none. The cruiser was pecked with holes.

The sun glistened off the snow, and Ivan guessed it would be in Ladd's eyes. He had enough ammo to last a good while, but more police would be here soon; if he had any chance at all, he had to move now. Still on his belly, he loaded the shotgun. Then he opened the passenger door, climbed over Dmitri and dropped into the snow. He crept around the back of the truck, tasting the blood in his throat. He snorted and spit, the blood a pure red in the white of the snow. It has come to this, he thought. It felt surreal; that Dmitri was dead and that likely he was too; that his life would end this way, out of his control; how he'd lived in control, always, but now everything had gotten away from him so quickly. He thought of Joseph, and wondered if he was praying for him now. Then high up in the sky his eye caught the moon, still out, and he knew that that was real; that it was as real as anything. It did not belong there, and neither did he. He looked down at the shotgun and took a deep breath. Then he stepped out from behind the truck, the shotgun at his hip, and dashed toward the cruiser and fired, shattering the windshield, then pumped the gun and fired again.

Ladd emerged, not from the front of the cruiser where Ivan had expected, but from the rear, which gave him just enough time to aim and fire three quick shots that hit Ivan squarely in the chest and killed him instantly.

A cold wind blew across the field and over the road, whistling softly through the trees. The gunshots were ringing in Ladd's ears. It took him a moment to realize the tranquility around him, the sudden peacefulness, but once he did he sat in the snow, the sun on his face, and breathed. It wasn't long before he heard the murmur of sirens in the distance.

Chapter 23

Prin rushed through King Square, bag in hand, a swarm of pigeons scattering in her wake. She hated being late. She hurried as fast as she could, careful not to fall as she made her way down King Street and into Brunswick Square. She regretted not going to April's first to see Daisy; that April had said she'd take care of her and for her not to worry. She skipped down the escalator two steps at a time, then across the eatery and into the washrooms. She hated changing in such a tight space, but there really was no other place for her to do this; that this bathroom had seen her transform herself into someone new so many times that it had become a safe place to her; a place that knew and kept her secrets without judgment. She nearly tripped over the toilet, trying to hang her dress on the hook. Then, in her stockings, she stepped in a wet spot on the floor and cursed. Two minutes later she exited the stall, plopped her makeup bag on the counter and applied eyeliner, lipstick, and put a clip in her hair, pressing her bangs to her forehead. When she was finished she stepped back and looked at herself in the mirror and tingled with joy. The flowered summer dress, though out of season, hung to her knees and brightened her whole body, like the flowers in her window. She placed a daisy in her hair, behind her ear, wrapped herself in her coat again and stepped out into the eatery, confident; it was in her strut, no longer uneven, but now sure of itself, moving her along with such grace she seemed to glide.

She skipped up the escalator to the main floor, then outside and down King Street. Charlie and two others were waiting outside City Hall.

Charlie was wearing a tuxedo. A tuxedo! She hurried her pace. You're really doing this, she thought. She couldn't help but giggle to herself. Charlie handed her a bouquet of flowers and her eyes started to water.

"You remember Shawn," Charlie said.

Shawn shook Prin's hand very business-like; a firm handshake.

"From the Bourbon Quarter," Prin said.

Shawn nodded and smiled, then stepped aside.

"This is my wife, Jess."

Jess, big eyed and smiling, shivered in the cold. She handed Prin a tissue to wipe the mascara that had started to run.

"Forgive me," Jess said. "But I thought Charlie was making this whole thing up."

April and Daisy arrived a few minutes later. Prin picked up Daisy and kissed her cheek.

"Oh Charlie, she's beautiful," Jess said.

Charlie gave Daisy a quick peck on the cheek, which confused her, but she liked the attention she was getting, with everyone looking at her. April had taken her to Walmart and had bought her a brand new dress and she was enjoying being a real princess today. The cars passed through the intersection, exhausts smoking in the cold.

"I didn't think we could do this on a Saturday," Prin said.

"I know a guy," Shawn said, and winked.

Charlie was smiling.

"He knows a guy." He took Prin by the arm. "You ready for this?"

Forty minutes later they stepped outside. Charlie was holding the marriage certificate.

"Now what?" Prin said, smiling and chuckling, and so giddy she didn't feel the cold through her sundress.

"Brunch," Shawn said. "Everything should be just about ready."

They crossed the intersection and onto Prince William Street and into the Bourbon Quarter where a local jazz band greeted them. The warm aromas made their mouths water; deep fried French toast with cinnamon, vanilla and whipped cream, buttermilk waffles, peppered maple bacon, sausages, homefries, beignets, English muffins, fruit, and omelettes with chorizo, jalapenos and garlic. A table was set up by the front window with daisies and champagne.

Shawn lifted his glass.

"To Charlie and Prin," he said. "May you live long, and most importantly, happily ever after. And Prin, a word of advice: If you've got any Harlequin Romances at home, I suggest you throw them out."

It took the rest of the afternoon for Charlie and Shawn to get the snow off Charlie's roof; it was a hard crusted snow and they had to chip away at it and remove it in big chunks, dropping it over the side of the building into the alley. Prin had gone out and bought Christmas lights and they ran them from one end of the roof to the other, forming a canopy of lights. They lugged the speakers from the Bourbon Quarter and hooked up an iPad and let it play. They also brought two huge heat lamps Shawn used for his patio in the fall. They ordered pizzas and chicken wings and bought wine and beer and had everyone from the building come up and celebrate. Murray from the first floor brought an ice cream cake. Mrs. Fisher from 2B brought fresh bread and a lasagna from Vitos. Ed and Louisa, who'd lived in the building since 1968, brought a tray of Rice Krispy squares, which Daisy ate too many of and went downstairs to bed with a sore tummy. The only person missing was Jeremy Wiggins, who hadn't answered his door all day.

Charlie was still in his tuxedo, the bottoms of his trousers frozen, but Prin had changed from her dress into pants and the wool coat with the big red buttons that Charlie had thought she'd looked so pretty in yesterday. They leaned over the ledge, their backs to the party.

"Did we do the right thing, Charles?"

"Of course," Charlie said. "You're not quitting on me already, are you?"

"No. I just worry."

"Don't," Charlie said. "I'm happy. Are you happy?"

"I am, yes," she said.

"Then that's all that matters."

People were dancing and laughing behind them.

"But what about tomorrow?" Prin said. "Or next week, or next month, or next year—once reality sets in? Marriage isn't easy."

"Reality's overrated," Charlie said.

"It's just so crazy," Prin said. "I mean, we actually did this." A warmth swept over her, and she smiled, trying to absorb it, not knowing how long it would last, how long any of this would last—this delicate thing she and Charlie now shared—real or not—but it made her feel warm inside and that's all she cared about. She looked out over the rooftops, to the black of the harbour, and she smiled again. "Look, Charles," she said. "Look at the moon—you can see it in the water. Isn't it lovely?"

The End

Thank You

Leigh
Hadley
Harper
D.A. Lockhart
Bethany Gibson
Dilshad Engineer
David Adams Richards
Ian Colford
Lee D. Thompson
Rod Anstee
Clive Baugh

About the Author

Jerrod Edson was born in Saint John, New Brunswick, in 1974. He is a graduate of Carleton University and York University. He lives in Mississauga, Ontario, with his wife Leigh, and daughters Hadley and Harper. *The Moon is Real* is his fifth novel.

Also Available from Urban Farmhouse Press

Ash (*Kilgore Trout Series*) by Kelly Dulaney, ISBN: 978-0-9937690-6-1

The Burning Hour (*UFP Fiction*) by Jessica Inclan Barksdale, ISBN: 978-1-9882140-4-7

Booking Rooms in the Kuiper Belt (*Crossroads Poetry Series*) by Kenneth Pobo, ISBN: 978-0-993769-07-8

Curious Connections (*Cities of the Straits Chapbook*) by Karen Rockwell, ISBN: 978-1-988214-07-8

Endless Building (*Crossroads Poetry Series*) by Marvin Shackelford, ISBN: 978-0-993769-01-6

Home & Ghost (*Crossroads Poetry Series*) by Scott Weaver, ISBN: 978-1-988214-05-4

Jesus Works the Night Shift (*Cities of the Straits Chapbook*) by Caleb Tankersley, ISBN: 978-0-993769-02-3

Legacy (*Vintage Sci-Fi*) by Larry Schmitz, ISBN: 978-1-988214-03-0

Puppet Turners of Narrow Interior (*UFP Fiction*) by Stephanie Hammer Barbe, ISBN: 978-0-993769-03-0

Roundabout Directions to Lincoln Center (*Crossroads Poetry Series*) by Renee K. Nicholson, ISBN: 978-0-993769-01-6

Smack in the Middle of Spotlit Obvious (*Cities of the Straits Chapbook*) by Laurie Smith, ISBN: 978-1-988214-06-1

Other Books by Jerrod Edson

The Goon (Oberon Press, 2010)

A Place of Pretty Flowers (Oberon Press, 2007)

The Dirty Milkman (Oberon Press, 2005)

The Making of Harry Cossaboom (DreamCatcher Publishing, 2000)

CPSIA information can be obtained
at www.ICGtesting.com
ted in the USA
W12s0327181016
173LV00004B/6/P